P9-CIW-118

FIRE ON HEADLESS MOUNTAIN

FIRE ON HEADLESS MOUNTAIN

IAIN LAWRENCE

MARGARET FERGUSON BOOKS
HOLIDAY HOUSE • NEW YORK

Margaret Ferguson Books

Printed and bound in June 2022 at Maple Press, York, PA, USA.
www.holidayhouse.com
First edition
1 3 5 7 9 10 8 6 4 2
Library of Congress Cataloging-in-Publication Data
Names: Lawrence, Iain, 1955- author.
Title: Fire on Headless Mountain / Iain Lawrence.
Description: First edition. | New York City : Holiday House, [2022]. | Audience: Ages 9 to 12. | Audience: Grades 4-6. | Summary: Eleven-year-old Virgil Pepper is returning to Little Lost Lake in Oregon with his older brother and sister to scatter their mother's ashes in the place she loved best, but when their van breaks down in the middle nowhere, it is up to Virgil, who shared his mother's love of science and the wild, to remember and use all the lessons she taught him to survive a forest fire started by a lightning strike.
Identifiers: LCCN 2021036081 | ISBN 9780823446544 (hardcover)
Subjects: LCSH: Forest fires—Juvenile fiction. | Survival—Juvenile fiction. Mothers and sons—Juvenile fiction. | Brothers and sisters—Juvenile fiction. Grief—Juvenile fiction. | Oregon—Juvenile fiction. | CYAC: Forest fires—Fiction. Survival—Fiction. | Mothers and sons—Fiction. | Brothers and sisters—Fiction. Grief—Fiction. | Oregon—Fiction. | LCGFT: Novels.
Classification: LCC PZ7.L43545 Fi 2022 | DDC 813.54 [Fic]—dc23/eng/20211018
LC record available at https://lccn.loc.gov/2021036081
ISBN: 978-0-8234-4654-4 (hardcover)

For Annie

FIRE ON HEADLESS MOUNTAIN

DAY ONE

1

On the Boneyard

Down through the valley of the Bigfoot River runs a road called the Boneyard. Eighty miles of dirt and gravel as cratered as the moon, it snakes through the forest to Little Lost Lake, where the water is robin-egg blue.

The Peppers had gone there every summer for as long as Virgil could remember. Little Lost Lake was his mother's favorite place in the whole world, and it was there that she had taught him how to use the stars for a compass, how to paddle a canoe and make a fire without a match—all those wonderful things that only bored his father.

"Make me a promise," she had said when she was dying. "Scatter my ashes on Little Lost Lake."

It was a blistering day in August when the Pepper children went back down the Boneyard to carry out that last wish. Their father had asked if they'd go without him, and then had flown to a writer's conference in San Francisco to make sure he was far away. "I just can't go back there," he'd told them. "Not now nor ever, I think. I'm sorry, kids, but this is something you're going to have to do by yourselves."

Joshua was happy with that. He was nineteen, but he'd had his driver's license for less than three months. He had never driven the old Westfalia camper van they called Rusty, but his father had told him not to worry. "You'll do just fine. You're in good hands with Rusty."

As they turned off the highway and onto the Boneyard, Joshua drove even slower than his dad would have done. He gripped the wheel with both hands and dodged round the potholes. But no matter how carefully he drove, the van rattled down the road like an old tricycle, banging over the rough spots.

Kaitlyn, the middle child, was playing music on her iPhone. In shorts and a tank top, sprawled in the passenger's seat beside Joshua, she bobbed her head to the booming in her earbuds.

In the back sat Virgil. The shadows of the trees flickered across his face as he stared out at the forest going by. In two weeks he'd turn twelve, but he was small for his age, as thin as a stick figure, and everyone thought he was younger.

In years past, the Peppers had laughed their way down the Boneyard, singing songs and playing silly games. Now they traveled for miles without saying a word, only three of them where there'd always been five. They were nearly twenty miles from the highway before anyone spoke. It was Joshua, calling out above the racket from the van.

"Hey, look at those clouds."

Virgil turned his head. Through the windshield, he saw the flattened top of Headless Mountain rising above the trees like the hump on a grizzly bear. Enormous clouds churned above it in shades of yellow and gray.

"They look foreboding," said Joshua. Like his dad, he often used fancy words and colorful phrases. Sometimes Kaitlyn teased him about it, but all he would do was laugh—just as his dad would have done. Leaning forward over the steering wheel, he gazed at the churning sky. "What kind are they, Virg?" he asked.

"Cumulonimbus!" cried Virgil. He knew every type of cloud, from stratus to cirrus, and this was his favorite. "They might be ten miles high. Maybe more. They could be—"

"What do they mean?" Joshua interrupted.

"There's going to be an electrical storm." Virgil sounded excited. "Those are thunderheads, Josh! They're lightning factories."

He had always loved science. When he was four years old, his favorite bedtime book was *Atom Alphabet*. At six, he was making strange machines out of things he found around the house. His father jokingly called him Leonardo da Virgil.

"I'm getting goose bumps," said Kaitlyn. She pulled out her earbuds and rubbed her arms fiercely. "It feels prickly."

"That's ozone!" Virgil had to shout above the noise of the road and the rattle of the van. "It's made by lightning. So when you smell a storm coming, that's the ozone. And you know what else?"

It was their mother who'd taught him the science of storms, and he was eager to share what he'd learned. But as though he'd commanded it, the sky suddenly exploded in a flash of light. The clouds gleamed like yellow lanterns, then faded and gleamed again.

"Fantastic!" said Joshua.

Silently, Virgil started counting. One, steamboat. Two, steamboat. The thunder came as he reached thirty-nine, a low rumble that made him shiver happily. He divided the number by five and announced, "That was eight miles away!"

Kaitlyn glanced back at him. "Don't worry, Virg. It's not going to hurt us."

Virgil wasn't worried. It thrilled him to think of electrical charges racing across the sky, of the clouds becoming colossal batteries. He wanted to drive right through the middle of the storm and see it all around him, to feel the thunder booming in his chest.

As the clouds churned above the mountain, flaring with lightning bolts, Joshua slowed the van to watch the storm. He said, "Oh, I wish Mom could see this."

And that changed everything.

With a sigh, Virgil flopped back in his seat. He heard the wheels grinding over the gravel, taking him deeper into the valley with every turn, closer and closer to Little Lost Lake.

His mom had loved everything wild and exciting, but she had loved storms most of all. If she still was alive, if she was with them right then, she would be turned in her seat to face them, talking about the storm with her voice full of excitement and her hands making shapes in the air. She would be explaining why the clouds were oozing over the mountain like mustard gas, how the thunder made its ominous sounds. And she would make it so interesting that even Kaitlyn would start asking questions—and no one cared less about science than Kaitlyn.

That lack of interest had been a big disappointment for Virgil's mom, though she'd never said so. With a pang, Virgil remembered the look on her face when Kaitlyn's words had hurt her. It had been only a year before, on his mom's last trip down the Boneyard.

– – –

It's a rainy morning at Little Lost Lake. They're all huddled inside the van, and the windows are wet with the fog from their breathing. Water blown from the trees is drumming down on Rusty's pop-up roof. On the back seat, Kaitlyn and Joshua are playing War with a deck of cards. In the front, Dad has swiveled the driver's seat to work on a little watercolor painting on the swing-out table. The tip of his tongue pokes out between his lips.

Mom wipes the window with the red-handled squeegee they call the "vindow-viper." It squeals across the glass with a sound that makes Virgil cringe. Then she peers out at the rain, at the treetops bending in the wind. "I think it's time," she says. "You ready, Virg?"

"Sure," says Virgil. He's already bundled up in his yellow rainsuit.

Mom tightens the drawstring on her day pack and hoists it up onto one shoulder. "Do you want to come along, Josh?"

"No, thanks," says Joshua.

"Kait?"

Kaitlyn doesn't even look up from the cards. "I'd rather stick pins in my eyes."

Mom looks disappointed. It's only for an instant, but it hurts Virgil to see the twitch in her mouth, the sad blink in her eyes. Then she's smiling again, as happy as ever. "Well, I guess it's just you and me, Virgil," she says, and out they go into the rising storm.

Down at the lake the wind is whipping the water into tiny spikes. The trees bend and bow, and tiny twigs torn from their branches go tumbling past without touching the ground.

Mom kneels on the wet grass and empties her pack. She pulls out things that make no sense: an empty jar and a red balloon, a needle, a roll of tape, a straw, and a rubber band. Then she takes those things and builds a barometer.

Virgil watches her hands. Red with cold on this summer morning, they stretch the balloon across the mouth of the jar to make a flexible lid. They snap the rubber band around it to hold it in place, then fix the needle to one end of the straw. They lay the other end across the balloon and tape it down. The straw becomes a lever, with the edge of the jar for its fulcrum.

"Now we watch," says Mom when she's finished.

Like a pointing finger, the needle at the end of the straw moves steadily downward.

"That's the storm coming closer," says Mom. "The air pressure's falling, so the atmosphere inside the jar is pushing up on the balloon."

The needle drops a quarter inch in half an hour, then begins to rise again as the storm moves on. The wind that had gusted and roared begins to calm down. Shafts of sunlight spear through the clouds.

"It always gets brighter when a storm passes over," says Mom. Suddenly she's serious, staring right into his eyes. "Listen, Virgil, don't ever forget that. No matter how bad the storm, it always gets sunny again."

– – –

Virgil was suddenly shaken out of his memory as Rusty bounced over ruts in the Boneyard. Aware again of the trees going by and the pulsing roar of the engine, he thought of what his mom had said that day and decided she'd been wrong. There had been a storm inside him ever since she'd died, and he didn't believe it would ever pass over. He could not imagine a day when he would be ready to go on without his mother.

It didn't seem so hard for the others. Joshua had left right after the funeral to study Spanish in Costa Rica. Kaitlyn kept herself busy with sports, going out every evening to play some sort of game. But Virgil hadn't known his mom for as long as the others, and he felt cheated by that. She had started teaching at his middle school just one year before he got there, so neither Kaitlyn nor Joshua had been in her class. He had loved to see her breezing down the hall with a huge smile on her face, every kid calling out, "Hi, Mrs. Pepper" or "Good morning, Mrs. Pepper."

And then there was his dad, who didn't understand at all. Every day and every night, just as he'd always done, he closed the door to his writing room and worked in a din of classical music. "We don't have to pretend that nothing has changed," he'd told Virgil. "Our happiness has been snatched away, and our lives will never be the same. But wallowing in sadness won't help anybody. We have to shake ourselves out of our terrible dream and keep living."

But to Virgil, that was impossible. When summer ended, he would start seventh grade in the same school. He would hear all over again the whispering behind him wherever he went, and the endless, hollow things that people said to help him: "I bet you miss your mom a lot." "I can't believe she's gone." Every morning, he would walk past her science room. Every afternoon, he would play on the field where his whole class had spent a rainy hour making those crazy barometers that she had tried out first on him. He had always been her guinea pig, and he missed that most of all.

Before he knew it, Virgil was crying. Silently, unashamed, he let tears spill from his eyes. They tickled on his skin as though flies were walking down his cheeks, but he didn't try to wipe them away. He just stared blankly through the window as lightning flickered over Headless Mountain.

One peal of thunder rumbled right into the next one. Joshua cried out in Spanish, "*Ay, caramba!*"—making Kaitlyn laugh.

With everywhere to look at once, only Virgil saw the one long bolt of lightning that zigzagged through the clouds. Thin and spidery, dazzled by his tears, it went sizzling down behind Headless Mountain. At almost the same moment another flare of light appeared, as though a giant had struck a match along the mountain's ragged ridge.

A crack of thunder and a shuddering boom followed seconds later. Virgil had always loved that sound.

He remembered asking his parents about it. And again he was carried back into his memories.

– – –

He's so small that he can sit on his father's bent arm like a ventriloquist's doll. His pudgy hands are pressed against the living room window, and he's looking out through tiny rivers of rain that run down the glass. Outside, lightning is flashing in a dark sky.

"Dad, what makes the thunder?"

"Monsters," his dad tells him. "Big thunder monsters thumping around on the clouds."

"Really?" he asks. "Do they live up there? Do they have houses?"

"Houses? Now you're being silly," says his dad. "They live in castles, of course. Great cloudy castles with yellow flags on the turrets."

Virgil looks up at the night sky, at the clouds that appear in the flashes of lightning.

"Of course," says Dad, smiling, "your mother would tell you something different."

So Virgil turns to her and asks, "What's thunder, Mom?" And she answers matter-of-factly, "It's an explosion of super-heated air compressed by lightning."

– – –

Virgil came out of his memory with a sniff and a smile. That was the last time he'd ever gone to his dad with a question about science. It was different if he wanted to know about words or books or big ideas, but he'd never trusted his father again about things like thunder and lightning.

His father was a writer who made the world seem wonderfully magical. But his mother had never lied to him.

Virgil sniffed again. At last he rubbed his eyes, pressing hard with his knuckles, trying to squeeze out the tears.

There was no more lightning after that last, unusual flash on the mountain, and no more booming thunder. The road began to turn in a long, slow curve and Headless Mountain slipped away behind the trees. The clouds broke apart, and patches of blue sky appeared between them. Before long, the day was again sunny and hot, and nobody talked in the van.

They went over a rise and plunged into the darkness of the forest. The trees closed around them, hiding the sky and the mountain. Joshua steered through a tunnel of trees until they burst out into sunshine on the crest of a hill. For the next forty miles it would be the same thing, into the forest and out again, from sunshine to darkness to sunshine again, all the way to Little Lost Lake.

Virgil wondered about the flash of light he'd seen. Ball lightning? A superbolt? He wished he could ask his mother about it, as he had asked so many times about so many things. The thought reminded him of the little wooden box on the shelf above his head, the tiny ark that held his mother's ashes, and the strange light vanished from his mind.

2

The Lightning Strike

The lightning storm sparked seven fires in the fifty miles around Headless Mountain. Thunder was still booming in the valley as hotshot crews headed off to fight them.

They started with the ones that threatened homes and buildings, the ones that were easy to reach, the ones that a helicopter could put out with a single bucket of water. But they didn't need to fight them all.

Fires are good for the forests. They clean out the old, dead wood and make room for new growth. Just as people build new cities on top of old ones, forests flourish on the ashes of others. So a few are left to burn for days or weeks at a time.

The most remote of those seven fires began with the last lightning bolt that Virgil had spotted through Rusty's windshield. On the other side of Headless Mountain, in the valley he couldn't see, a giant tree was burning.

It was a Douglas fir as old as America. When Paul Revere set out on his midnight ride, it was a sapling with a trunk as thin as a finger. By the time Virgil was born, it was as tall as a building with twenty-five stories. Centuries of fire, wind, and snow had blackened its bark and chopped away its limbs. A survivor of summer drought and winter storms, of fire, flood, and plague, it had seemed immortal—until the lightning struck.

A billion volts of electricity shot through the tree, and in that instant it exploded. The branches blew off; the top sheared away; the trunk split open for a hundred feet. Inside, the sap began to boil, and clouds of steamy smoke wrapped around the tree like the windings of a mummy.

Though nearly chopped in half, the tree was still standing. Deep inside the splintered trunk, yellow flames flickered at the dark core known as the heartwood. A column of old, dead cells stronger than steel, it made up the backbone of the tree. If the storm brought rain, or if firefighters arrived in time, the tree could still survive.

But if the flames ate through the heartwood, it would soon come crashing down.

3

Old Rusty

Kaitlyn kicked off her sandals and plonked her bare feet on the dashboard. Her skin was darkly tanned, tattooed with white strips where the sandal straps had been. Her toes reminded Virgil of little brown sausages, and he cringed at the sight of them pressing against the windshield. His mom had sat in that same way in that same place, and the soles of her sneakers had printed checkerboard patterns on the glass. They were still there, though as faint as tire tracks on a rainy road, and Virgil didn't want anything to rub them away.

Kaitlyn wriggled her toes, rubbing those little sausages against the windshield. Virgil wanted to yell at her, "Don't do that!" But he knew she wouldn't understand. She would turn toward Joshua with that look Virgil hated, the smile that said, Do you think Virgil will ever grow up?

He looked away. Through the window above the tiny

sink, he stared at the blur of trees going by. Every three minutes a yellow sign with black numbers appeared, counting the miles from the highway.

At Mile 24, Joshua picked up the imaginary microphone of an imaginary CB radio. "Breaker, breaker," he said. "This is Big Virgil."

From Kaitlyn he got a grin and a bright little laugh. But Virgil only groaned.

Every year it was the same thing. Somewhere along the Boneyard, Joshua clicked that imaginary microphone and reminded everyone of the time that Virgil had pretended to be a logging-truck driver. With a paper plate for a steering wheel, he had guided his big rig down the road from Rusty's back seat, calling out the miles as the signs went by, warning oncoming trucks that he was coming. His microphone had been a potato peeler, his gear shift a wooden spoon. At the time, it had seemed as real as his memories. He'd imagined the thundering roar of a big Cummins diesel; the answering crackle over his radio from another driver roaring toward him loaded with logs; the throttling sound of his engine brake as he edged over to let the other truck go by. Now it embarrassed him to think about it.

With every sign that passed, they were another mile farther from the highway, another mile deeper into the wilderness. At Mile 28, he began to worry. He remembered a sentence he'd read in a book just two days before; he heard it in his head.

"People go into that valley and disappear."

The passing trees became a hypnotizing blur, and Virgil's eyes took on a faraway look as he slipped into his memories.

– – –

Kaitlyn is in the living room, stretched out on the couch with a book in her hands. The TV is on, blaring laughter from a sitcom, but she's not watching it.

"What are you reading?" he asks.

She tilts the book just enough to let him see the cover. The title is written in huge red letters: Blood in the River.

"What's it about?"

"How Headless Mountain got its name."

"Oh, everyone knows that," he says. "It looks like the top was cut off."

"Wrong."

"That's what Mom told me."

"I know. She told me that too. But it's still wrong."

He holds out his hand for the book. "Let me see."

"No." Kaitlyn pulls it closer to her chest. "You don't want to read this, Virg."

"Why?"

"You'll have nightmares."

He scoffs. "Yeah, right."

"Seriously. I know how you are. You'll never want to go there again."

The more Kaitlyn tells him not to read the book, the more he wants to see inside it. But she doesn't give him a chance until that evening, when she goes out with Josh to meet their friends.

Upstairs, violin music is wailing from the study. Virgil's dad is locked up in there, writing poetry or something. As quietly as he can, Virgil opens the door to Kaitlyn's bedroom. He slips inside and closes it softly, holding the handle so the latch won't make a sound.

He finds the book on her nightstand and sits on the bed to read it. On the back is a blurb in capital letters.

> AN EMPTY TENT WITH ITS SIDE TORN OPEN. A DEAD MAN WARMING HIS HANDS AT A FIRE. TERRIFYING SCREAMS IN THE NIGHT.
>
> THESE ARE THE STORIES OF HEADLESS MOUNTAIN AND THE RIVER CALLED THE BIGFOOT. SOMETHING SINISTER LURKS IN THE VALLEY WHERE THE BIGFOOT FLOWS. PEOPLE HAVE TRIED TO EXPLAIN THE STRANGE SOUNDS AND STRANGE SIGHTS. BUT ONLY ONE THING IS KNOWN FOR SURE.
>
> PEOPLE GO INTO THAT VALLEY AND DISAPPEAR.

He knows his sister is right. If he reads the book, he'll be sorry. But now he can't stop himself. He cracks it open warily, knowing that something will leap from the pages and scare him.

He finds that thing right away, in a blurry picture and a startling caption. "The way a person hunts animals, a Sasquatch hunts people."

That word has always frightened him: Sasquatch. Half

man, half ape, standing nine feet tall, it bounds from the book and into Virgil's imagination. Every page he turns to holds a new fright that he knows he'll never forget.

"It dragged her out of the tent feet first. It hauled her into the forest, into the darkness. She was screaming."

"I never heard anything like that before, and I hope I never hear it again."

"It tore off his head. Pssht! Like twisting a cap from a bottle."

– – –

A yellow flash in Virgil's window shocked him from his memory. But he turned his head too late to read the number, and it seemed forever until the next sign appeared. Mile 30.

Eleven miles to go, he thought. At Mile 41 they would cross Trickleback Creek, where Kaitlyn's book had begun with the most frightening story of all. They would rumble over the old log bridge that his mom had hated so much, and he would feel safer then, with the creek behind them.

"It was at Trickleback Creek that the killing started."

The words from Kaitlyn's book still haunted him; he thought they always would.

"When the sun went down the thing came back. One by one it killed them all."

Virgil didn't want to think about it. He watched for the mile markers as Rusty barreled down the Boneyard in its cloud of dust. The sign at Mile 31 was peppered by shotgun pellets, and the next was twisted and bent. "Nine more miles to go," said Virgil to himself. Behind his seat, under the cushions of the folding bed, below a metal cover, the engine clattered away with its throaty roar. But Virgil found comfort in the sound. It made his closed-in world feel warm and safe. Until they passed Mile 33. Then Virgil heard a tiny click he'd never heard before. No louder than a snapping twig, it seemed to him as alarming as a gunshot.

"I think something's wrong with the engine," he shouted.

Joshua peered at the gauges on the dashboard. "It looks okay," he said.

"But—"

"Come on, Virg, it's good old Rusty."

That was what their father always said. The van had taken them thirty thousand miles across twenty-two states, and at the end of each trip he'd patted its side and told them, "Good old Rusty. He's going to run forever." But Virgil had learned every sound the engine made, every tick, every tock, every rattle and jingle. And he knew that tiny click was just not right.

At Mile 34 he smelled a sweet hotness that tickled his throat. When he looked back he saw a whorl of mist rising from the engine compartment.

"Josh!" he yelled. "It's smoking!"

Joshua's face appeared in the rearview mirror, and his eyes suddenly widened. On the dashboard a red light started flashing, and Kaitlyn cried out at the same moment, "You'd better stop!"

"I can't," said Joshua. "Not here."

The road was cut into a hillside, with the forest falling away on the left. On the right the foliage pressed in close to the road, leaving no room to pull over. Joshua kept his foot on the gas, his hands on the wheel, guiding Rusty round a curve.

"There!" shouted Kaitlyn. She pointed ahead at a small gravel pit bulldozed into the slope.

It came up suddenly. Joshua jammed his foot on the brake pedal and spun the steering wheel. Rusty skidded sideways toward the gravel pit and shuddered to a stop at the edge of the road.

Virgil unfastened his seat belt, flung open the sliding door, and tumbled out like a soldier from a helicopter.

The heat of the sun baking down on the Boneyard took his breath away. He looked at Rusty and groaned. "Josh, you'd better come and see this," he said.

A puddle was oozing out from under the van. Black and steamy, it might have been an alien creature trying to crawl across the gravel. When Joshua saw it, he clamped his head in his hands and groaned.

"Can you fix it?" asked Virgil.

"I don't know." Joshua stood in the sunshine with his hands on his head, as though he'd already surrendered. Under his arms, sweat stains made big moon shapes on his T-shirt. "I guess I'd better take a look."

He walked to the back of the van, opened the hatch, and shoved the cushions aside. When he lifted the lid from the engine compartment, waves of heat shimmered around him, stinking of antifreeze and hot oil. For a moment he staggered backward, then he stepped forward again and leaned over the engine.

"There's oil all over the place," he said. "It's like the engine blew up or something."

To Virgil, watching from behind, his brother could have been a surgeon bending over a patient. When Joshua thrust his hands down among Rusty's rubber intestines, Virgil actually believed for a second that he would heal the old van.

But as Joshua poked at the battery cables and jiggled the wires, Virgil realized that that would never happen. Wanting to help, he got down on his knees at the back of the van and leaned underneath to study the engine.

"Get up," said Joshua. "That stuff's poisonous. It kills dogs."

"But I can see where it's leaking out," said Virgil.

"Where?"

"Right here. Look."

Joshua knelt beside Virgil. He peered into the shadows under the van, at a trickle of oil and water dribbling down from the engine. In Spanish he said, "*Ay, maldito.*"

Virgil didn't know any Spanish. "What does that mean?" he asked.

"It means I can't fix it."

"Why?"

"Because it's no good. It's a piece of junk."

With a sigh, Virgil stood up and walked away. His brother and his father had a lot of things in common: not only a love of language and a deep laugh, but a short fuse as well. For both, it was always quick to fizzle out. But when either sounded frustrated, the best thing to do was leave him alone for a while.

At the side of the road, where it bulged out into the gravel pit, Kaitlyn was jabbing at the screen of her iPhone. She smiled at Virgil as he came up beside her. "Don't feel bad," she said. "He's mad at the van, not at you."

"Yeah, I know," said Virgil. He kicked at the gravel, stirring dust with his toes. "I wish Uncle Birdy was here."

He didn't mean for his brother to hear him. But Joshua got up from the road with his knees all dusty, tiny grains of gravel stuck in the palms of his hands, and he told Virgil, "Birdy couldn't fix it. Nobody can."

"Why?" asked Kaitlyn. She spoke gently, calmly, in a little girl's voice. "What's wrong with it, Josh?"

"I don't know," said Joshua. "But it's bad."

"Could we still drive it?"

"We could *start* it," said Joshua. "It just wouldn't go very far."

"Why?" she asked, in the same quiet way. "What would happen?"

Exactly as his dad would have done, Joshua sighed and shrugged. "It would seize up for sure. It might even explode. I told you; it's junk."

"So what are we going to do?" asked Virgil.

"What do you think?" said Joshua. "We'll call Dad."

"Not from here." Kaitlyn held up her phone. "There's no signal."

"Oh, great," said Joshua. "Then I guess we just wait for someone to come along."

They stood in the middle of the dusty Boneyard, all three in a row with their shadows so black and perfect that there might have been six people there. All at once, they turned their heads to look up the road, then turned their heads to look down the road. Virgil imagined that his brother and his sister were thinking the same thing that he was thinking.

No one was going to come along.

4

The Lookout

On the other side of Headless Mountain, on the edge of the avalanche chute, a lookout tower poked high above the trees. With a wooden hut perched on four long legs, it looked as spindly as a Tinkertoy set down on the mountainside. Through sixty years of summer storms, a fire watcher had sat at the top with binoculars, scanning the valley for lightning strikes.

From there, the smoke from the burning tree was clearly visible. Pinned down by the high pressure of the summer air, it flowed through the treetops and tumbled slowly into the valley.

But there was no one at the lookout to see the smoke. It had been closed down at the end of the last fire season, decommissioned to save the cost of a fire watcher. The nearest people in any direction were the Peppers, and they were on the other side of Headless Mountain, nearly twenty miles away.

Unseen by anyone, the shattered tree spat fire like a sparkler. All along the heartwood, yellow flames stretched into the air. The whole top section—three times the height of a normal house—was toppling sideways. The wood creaked and splintered, flinging off embers that spiraled away in trails of smoke.

5

House of Horrors

Huge bluebottle flies buzzed back and forth above Virgil's head. He lay stretched out on Rusty's back seat, watching them tap at the windows. When he heard footsteps in the gravel, he turned his head to see his brother appear in the doorway.

Joshua's face was red and sweaty. "You should come outside," he said. "It's too hot in there."

Virgil didn't move. "It's not so bad."

"All right, suit yourself," said Joshua, too hot to argue. From his pocket he pulled out his cell phone. "I'm going to walk up the road and see if I can get a signal."

"I'll go with you!" cried Virgil, already rolling himself off the seat.

Joshua looked surprised. "I thought you wanted to stay here."

"I changed my mind," said Virgil.

But Joshua wouldn't take him along. "You'd better stay here with Kaitlyn," he said. "In case someone comes by."

Virgil watched his brother walk away up the Boneyard, so dwarfed by the wilderness that he looked smaller than a Lego man. The sky was open all around, but trees blocked the view in every direction. Only the very top of Headless Mountain rose above them, nearly hidden by branches. When Joshua vanished round the first bend in the road, Virgil felt a deep and sudden loneliness. He called out for his sister. "Hey, Kait?"

"Over here," she answered.

He had to look around to find her, shading his eyes from the sun. She had crossed the clearing and climbed up the slope to find shade below an alder tree. He walked closer.

"What do you want?" she asked.

"I was just thinking," he said. "What if nobody comes by? What will happen then?"

"Aw, Virg, don't worry about it. Those big logging trucks drive past here all the time."

"No, they don't. It's been days since one went by."

"You don't know that," she said. "One might have gone by an hour ago."

Virgil waved his hand toward the other side of the road. "Then why's there no dust in the trees? Why are there no tracks in the gravel?"

Kaitlyn stood up and walked to the edge of the slope. She stood with her hands on her hips, looking down at the road. It was obvious that he was right. Wherever the logging trucks went, they churned up clouds of dust that coated everything. But there was nothing on the grass or the bushes or the trees beyond them.

"We could be here forever," said Virgil.

"I don't think so," said Kaitlyn. "If no one comes by we can walk. It's only thirty miles to the highway."

"Thirty-four."

"Well, whatever," she said. "If we left first thing in the morning we'd get out before dark."

"What if we left right now?"

"You want to walk all night?"

No, he didn't want to do that at all. One way or another, they would have to spend a night on the Boneyard, and he would rather be inside the van than out in the forest with the creatures that hunted in darkness.

"How far is it to the Sasquatch museum?" he asked.

Kaitlyn laughed. "Not far enough."

"No, seriously," said Virgil.

"Yes, seriously," she said right back. "Don't even think of going there, Virgil."

"There might be a radio. Maybe a satellite phone."

"I don't care," said Kaitlyn. "If Mom was here, you wouldn't even ask about it."

Virgil knew she was right. His mother had hated the Sasquatch museum. "The house of horrors," she'd called it. "I wouldn't go inside that place for all the money in the world."

"It's not even a real museum," said Kaitlyn.

"I know that," said Virgil. It was an old ATCO trailer that

had probably been abandoned by loggers, just a guy living alone in the bush, as crazy as all the other guys who lived alone in the bush. Virgil's mother had called him the Bugaboo Man.

"It's so creepy." Kaitlyn shivered dramatically. "The skulls on the fence. The antlers and chainsaws and stuff. I think Mom was right; it's a psycho's place. I wouldn't go anywhere near it."

"But it's the only place where we might get help."

"We don't need any help," she said. "There's nothing to worry about, Virg."

That made him snort. There was plenty to worry about. Looking down the road, he talked to Kaitlyn with his back toward her. "People go into this valley and disappear."

She waited so long to answer that he finally turned around. Kaitlyn was staring at him. "You read my book," she said. "You actually went into my room and read that stupid book."

"It's not stupid," said Virgil.

"Sasquatches?"

"They're possible. Mom said so."

"She did not."

"You weren't there!" cried Virgil. "You don't know what she said."

"I know she wasn't scared of them." Kaitlyn sighed. "I told you not to read that book. I knew this would happen."

"People disappear," he said stubbornly. "Something hunts them down and kills them."

"Then it's probably the guy at the fake museum," said Kaitlyn. She wheeled around and went back to her place at the base of the tree. "That's what I'd worry about. A psychopath with a chainsaw. A maniac with a machete."

"Shut up," said Virgil. He didn't need anything more to keep him awake at night.

Feeling worried and angry, he sat down in Rusty's open doorway. His back was shaded, but the sun glared on his legs. In the terrible heat nothing moved except the flies, and they came around him in swarms—first the tiny blackflies that covered the backs of his hands like pepper from a shaker, then huge deerflies that swooped in one by one to take whole bites from his flesh before he even knew they'd landed. He chased them away by swinging his arms.

Virgil remembered his mom talking about flies, and his mind traveled back through time.

— — —

He's walking through the forest, a step behind his mother, down a trail that's used by bears. There's fresh scat colored red by berries, little heaps with flies crawling across them.

"Here's a bear's back scratcher," says Mom. She puts her hand on an old tree beside the trail. Around the trunk, the ground is hollowed into a little pit, and far above Virgil's head—farther even than his mother can reach—a clump of black fur is wedged in the bark.

Virgil imagines a bear standing there, its feet planted in the ground, rubbing its back up and down on the tree. It would have to be at least nine feet tall.

"Maybe we should turn around," he says.

"Soon," says Mom.

They go deeper into the forest. Virgil's mother is searching for the orange mushroom she calls "chicken of the woods," and he knows she'll never give up till she finds one. He's nervous, but she's not. Every few minutes, she calls out in a cheery voice. "Hello, bears. Just passing through."

"Maybe we should be quiet," says Virgil.

She smiles. "We don't want to surprise them, Virg. If they know we're coming they'll get out of our way. They don't want to hurt us."

"How do you know?"

"That's the way they are," she says. "Just because something's big doesn't mean it's dangerous. The tiniest creatures are the ones you have to worry about."

"Like what?"

"Viruses. Bacteria. You can't get any smaller than that," she says. "Out here, it's poisonous plants like the death cap. It's spiders and wasps. And flies. Flies are maybe the worst of all."

"'Cause they carry germs?"

"Well, I wasn't thinking of that," she says. "Sometimes people who get lost in the woods are driven insane by the flies. The sound of them. The biting. The scratching. People do crazy things when they can't get away from it. That's the biggest danger in this sort of country. If you lose your wits, you're dead."

– – –

"Here comes Josh," said Kaitlyn. "It looks like bad news."

Virgil surfaced from his memories as though from a pool of water, suddenly emerging into sunlight and sound. Kaitlyn had come down to the road without him even seeing her, and Joshua was trudging toward them. He looked as miserable as a football player coming off the field after a terrible loss.

When he was close, Kaitlyn called out. "No signal?"

Joshua shook his head. "Nope."

That was all he said, just that one word. He walked up to the van and went straight inside it. Virgil had to lean sideways to let him through the doorway.

"Did you try phoning?" asked Kaitlyn. "Sometimes you can call 911 even when there's no signal."

Joshua snapped at her from inside the van. "You think I don't know that?"

"Okay, I'm just trying to help," said Kaitlyn. She gave Virgil a funny little smile and whispered so quietly that he could hardly hear her. "We're going code yellow."

Virgil laughed. It was his mom who'd invented the codes that signaled Dad's moods: yellow for the first sign of annoyance when things were going wrong, red for the peevishness that was as close to rage as he ever got. There was a code blue that they talked about like a mythical thing that might exist but no one had ever seen. Even at code red, Dad was more funny than frightening. Virgil's mom had wondered once, "When your father's angry, does he remind you of Winnie-the-Pooh?"

With a clunk of metal and a grunt from Joshua, Rusty's

roof hinged open. Out fell a shower of dried leaves and pine needles that had been trapped there since the last camping trip. The struts locked with a bang; the canvas thrummed as it stretched into place. Virgil had always loved that little boom of cloth and steel, the sound of settling in at whatever campsite they'd chosen for the night. But now, on the lonely Boneyard, it scared him, and he looked up to see how far the sun had moved along. With trees all around, it had nearly reached the edge of the circle of sky above him.

Joshua rummaged noisily through the van. The cupboard doors banged open and shut. "Hey, Kaitlyn!" he yelled. "Where'd you put the food?"

Code red, thought Virgil. There was anger—and accusation—in his brother's voice. But Kaitlyn answered as calmly as ever. "You don't have to shout. I'm standing right here."

Joshua was a big kid with broad shoulders. The van rocked as he stepped into the doorway and poked his head outside. "Where's the food?" he said.

"Don't ask me," said Kaitlyn. "That was Virgil's job."

Virgil looked up with surprise. "What was my job?"

"Loading the coolers."

"Why was it *my* job?" he asked.

"Because I told you to do it," said Kaitlyn.

"You did not!"

"Virgil, I told you twice."

He could picture the coolers stacked neatly by the back door, the red one under the blue one, with a bulging bag of groceries balanced on top. But he didn't remember Kaitlyn telling him to carry them out to the van. Still, it was possible. When his sister told him what to do, he didn't always listen.

Joshua had no doubt who was right. He nudged Virgil with his knee and said, "Good job, Virg. Now we've got no food."

"It's not my fault!" said Virgil. Frustration made him shout, and for a moment all three of them were glaring at one another. But the Peppers never stayed angry for long, and—as usual—it was Kaitlyn who calmed things down. Maybe she saw the look on Virgil's face as he lowered his head and kicked at the gravel. Maybe she thought of their mother, always the peacemaker, who would have hated to see them angry.

"Well, there's nothing we can do about it now," she said. "There must be something in the cupboards."

"Oh, there is," said Joshua.

"What?"

"Snot in a can."

That made them laugh—first Kaitlyn, then Joshua, and finally Virgil as well—and it was just like the storm they'd seen over Headless Mountain, the thunder and lightning of their argument ending, their sky turning sunny again.

"Snot in a can" was Virgil's old name for cream of mushroom soup, a favorite of his mother, hated by everyone else. She took three or four cans on every camping trip, and it was a family joke to act disgusted when she ate it. But Virgil didn't feel like joking. Nobody did. In his mind, Virgil saw his mom pushing the last cans into the cupboard, her fingers encircling each one in turn, not knowing she would never touch them again.

The thought made him so sad that he felt his throat grow dry and lumpy. He got up to get himself a drink of water and stepped into the van to find every cupboard door hanging open, every drawer pulled out. Arranged on the counter were the three red cans, their tops measled with rust spots.

The van rocked again as Joshua stepped down to the road. He talked to Kaitlyn in a low voice, as though he didn't want Virgil to hear. "I've got a bad feeling, Kait. The van's as good as dead. We can't call for help. It's stinking hot. And now there's no food. I don't think it can get any worse."

But it could. And it did. Virgil stood over the sink, took a glass from the shelf, and pressed his foot on the pump switch. He heard the motor whirring behind the cupboards, but only a few drops of water spluttered from the tap.

He knew right away what that meant.

The tank was empty. They had no water.

6

The Spotter

The first person to see the Douglas fir burning on the other side of Headless Mountain was the spotter in a Cessna 180. As the pilot banked above it, he looked down at a broken giant lying in a field of fire.

Across the mountain and up the slope, in a circle around the fallen tree, a hundred acres of forest were burning. The spotter reported the fire by radio while the circling plane bobbled through air that churned with the updrafts. A dispatcher marked it on a map and looked for a nearby place to name it after. He chose the old abandoned lookout called Avalanche, and so the Avalanche Fire was born.

Every hotshot crew was busy somewhere else, leaving no one to send right away. High on a slope in an empty valley, more than fifteen miles from the nearest road, the Avalanche Fire posed no danger to anyone.

A decision was made—to let it run.

7

The Rule of Three

Virgil didn't tell anybody that the water tank was empty. Afraid he'd be blamed for that, as he'd been blamed for the missing food, he put his glass back on the shelf as quietly as he possibly could.

Even the tiny tap of it touching the wood seemed too loud, and his hand froze there as he glanced back to make sure that no one had heard. Side by side on the road, Joshua and Kaitlyn were looking at their cell phones.

The glass scraped softly across the wood as Virgil pushed it into place. It tilted in his fingers and tapped against another one with a tiny tingling sound that set his heart racing. But he got it straightened out, then quickly closed the cupboard door and turned around.

Joshua was right there, looking in through the doorway. He had his arms spread across it, and the tight sleeves of his black T-shirt stretched round his biceps. "What are you doing?" he asked.

"Nothing," said Virgil.

"You want to get me a drink of water?"

Virgil felt trapped, not sure what to do. In a small voice, he said, "I can't."

"Why not?" asked Joshua.

"There's no water."

"What do you mean there's no water?"

"I think the tank's empty."

"*Ay, caramba!*" Joshua stormed into the van, reached over Virgil's head, and pulled the same glass from the cupboard. "It's wet," he said.

"I know, I—"

"Move over." Joshua nudged Virgil aside and held the glass under the tap. When he pressed down on the switch, the motor whirred and the pump spluttered. To Virgil it was obvious that the tank was empty. But Joshua, being Joshua, tried again—and then again—tromping down on the pedal hard enough to rock the van. "You emptied the tank!" he said.

"It was already empty," said Virgil. "There was just a little bit that came out."

"Then why didn't you say something?"

"We were code yellow," said Virgil.

"Oh, grow up."

Virgil knew that his brother was upset, already worried about the van and the food and the heat. But it still stung to be told to grow up, to have his brother think of him as a helpless baby.

Joshua looked up at the sun, now touching the tops of the trees. "We'd better have a meeting," he said.

It was a family tradition to have a meeting when things were going wrong. But there had never been one without a parent, and Virgil had a funny feeling as he sat cross-legged on the gravel. He felt even younger than he was, as though his brother had become his father, his sister his mother.

Joshua brought an opened can of soup and three spoons in a little clutch, and the deer flies came with him, zooming round his hands. They settled on Virgil's spoon as he dipped it into the soup. They walked round the rim of the can, and when he chased them away, they only came right back again.

To Virgil, the soup was disgusting. As salty as seawater, warm and clotted, it was speckled with little bits of brown mushroom. He ate each glob with his eyes closed, hating the taste as it slid over his tongue, hating the feel of it clogging his throat.

"When we finish this, I'm going to walk the other way down the road and see if I can get a signal," said Joshua. "You guys should look for water."

"Where?" asked Virgil.

"I don't know." He gestured vaguely toward the trees. "In the forest."

He made it sound easy, as though they could walk a few yards from the road and find a quiet pool or a rushing stream. But Virgil knew it wasn't that simple. He could remember his mother telling him, "It's a lot easier to carry water into the forest than to look for it when you get there." Virgil passed the can of soup to Kaitlyn. She scooped out a spoonful and passed it on to Joshua. "What if we can't find any water?" she asked. "I think we should walk to Trickleback Creek."

"How far is that from here?" said Joshua.

Kaitlyn shrugged. "I don't know."

"Seven miles," said Virgil.

"So, fourteen altogether." Joshua scraped his spoon round the side of the can. "That's too far for a bucket of water. We wouldn't even get back before dark."

"It's going to be a clear night, and the moon's almost full," said Kaitlyn. "We could go there and stay till we're rescued."

"No!" said Virgil. That was the last thing he wanted to do. "We have to stay with the van. Anyway, it's so hot the creek might have dried up by now."

"Yeah, I guess that's true," said Joshua. He licked his spoon, then wiped his lips and passed the can to Virgil. "Remember how Mom hated Trickleback Creek?"

"Yeah, what was that all about?" asked Kaitlyn.

"I think it was the bridge she didn't like," said Joshua.

"Why?"

"'Cause it's too narrow. You have to go down the hill and round the curve, and you can't see what's coming."

"And there's no railing," said Virgil. "She always thought we'd go over the edge."

The can was almost empty, with just a gray glob at the bottom. Virgil offered it to Kaitlyn, but she only shook her head and wouldn't take it. Joshua, too, was finished. He took the can, collected the spoons, and carried them into the van. He came out with the yellow bucket that they still called "the new bucket," though it was more than five years old. It had replaced the red bucket that their father had broken when he'd tried to use it as a stepping stool. The black arrow that their mom had drawn on the side with a Sharpie was still there, pointing to the top. So was the message she'd thought was hilarious: THIS END UP.

Joshua put it down beside Rusty. "Try to fill it if you can," he said. "I'll be back before dark."

Virgil watched his brother walk away down the Boneyard, back the way they'd come. The sky was turning red with evening coming on, and it looked as though he was walking into flames.

Kaitlyn picked up the bucket. "I can look for water," she said. "Why don't you see if there's anything else in the van? Maybe Josh missed something."

That was fine with Virgil. He didn't want to go trekking through the darkening forest. As Kaitlyn went away with the bucket, he climbed back into the van. But though he searched through every space, through every cupboard and drawer, he could find nothing to eat or drink.

Kaitlyn didn't do much better. She came back with a handful of little red berries, but without a drop of water in the bucket.

"Everything's dried up," she said. "The trees are dying. The berries are hard as pebbles, most of them. These are the best I could find."

They were huckleberries peeled from the bush, mixed

with tiny scraps of leaves and twigs. Bowled in Kaitlyn's palm, they looked like a nest of tiny red eggs. She poured some into Virgil's hand, and he ate them one by one as he stared down the road.

"How far do you think he went?" asked Virgil.

Kaitlyn shrugged. "Who knows?"

Virgil heard a raven tapping in the forest. In a poem once, his father had compared the sound to the knock on a medium's table, "in the silence of the séance." He called the ravens "fortune-tellers caped in black feathers."

It was the same thing in *Blood in the River*. The ravens seemed to know when something bad would happen, and they appeared on whistling wings wherever a Sasquatch would come soon after. The campers at Trickleback Creek had tried to feed one before settling down for the night. Three hours later, the Sasquatch came.

"There was no warning. It ripped the tent wide open."

In a moment the story retold itself in Virgil's mind with every detail crystal clear. Then others followed in a dizzying blur of headless men and shaggy giants and howling from the forest. He kept gazing up the road, wondering what would happen if Joshua wasn't back before dark. What if they heard him calling from the forest, faintly and fearfully—"Virgil... Kaitlyn!"—and they had to go out there to find him? He couldn't imagine leaving the van behind and walking away among the trees.

As the sky darkened, the blackflies came thicker than ever. Then moths appeared, as pale as ghosts, and animals that had lain still in the heat of the day began to stir all around. They slithered on the ground and rustled through the bushes. A bat swooped by without a sound.

Kaitlyn changed into blue jeans. They had holes cut into the legs, and she worked her fingers inside them to scratch where bugs had bitten.

"You doing okay?" she asked.

Virgil nodded.

"We'll find water tomorrow," she said. "If there's mosquitoes, there's gotta be water somewhere."

"They can go three miles from their home," said Virgil.

Kaitlyn laughed. "How do you even know that?"

"I just know," said Virgil. It was one of those things he'd read in a book or seen in a documentary. Or his mom might have told him.

Virgil looked up at the sky. The first stars had started to appear, and a planet glowed in the fading blue above him. He said, "Did Mom ever tell you the rule of three?"

"You mean like how bad things come in threes?"

"No," he said. "She didn't believe in that sort of stuff. She told us in school one day."

He could remember the moment exactly, a spring day when the sun was shining through the blinds of the classroom windows, making crisscrossed shadows on the floor. His mother had stood at the front of the room with her legs hash marked by those shadows.

"She said a person can live three months without food, three days without water, and three minutes without air."

Kaitlyn didn't believe it. "Lots of people can hold their breath longer than three minutes," she said.

"I guess it's an average," said Virgil.

"And only three days without water?" Kaitlyn leaned back her head and sighed. "No way."

"That's what Mom said."

"Well, she wasn't always right, you know."

Virgil imagined how their mom would feel if she were sitting there, and a flash of anger and sadness and guilt ran through him all at once. "Don't say that!" he cried.

"Oh, Virg, it's all right," she said. "Nobody's perfect. Not even Mom."

Virgil turned away. So did Kaitlyn, a moment later, and they sat back-to-back in bitter silence until Virgil couldn't stand it anymore. "He's sure taking a long time," he said, meaning Joshua.

"Yeah. He is."

"You think he's okay?"

"Of course he's okay." She didn't sound worried at all. "Maybe he found a signal and he's sitting on a stump talking to Dad. Maybe he found someone camped along the road, and they're packing up right now to come and get us."

It was Kaitlyn's way to think of the good instead of the bad. Virgil was the opposite. Faced with a problem, he always went straight to what his mother had called "the dark side." He could imagine Joshua clinging to the top of a tree as a grizzly bear tried to shake him loose.

But, as usual, he was wrong. Joshua appeared a few minutes later, looking so weary that it was obvious he hadn't found a signal. He trudged up to the van and collapsed against it, leaning back with his eyes closed. "Did you get any water?"

"No," said Kaitlyn.

"Did you actually look?"

Code yellow, thought Virgil. Kaitlyn must have sensed it too, because she lowered her voice until she was barely whispering. "Yes, Josh, I looked."

"I just don't get it." Joshua banged his fist against the van, and it made a booming sound. "Dad filled up the gas and checked the oil. I can't believe he didn't fill the water tank too. He always does that."

"I guess he forgot," said Kaitlyn.

That gave Virgil an idea. He looked up and said, "Hey, Josh, do you think he remembered to dump out the waste water?"

"What difference does it make?" Josh hit the van again. "I should have checked the water myself. I should have looked."

Virgil felt that nobody ever listened to his ideas. He got up and walked away.

"Where are you going?" asked Kaitlyn.

"Nowhere," he said.

"It's getting dark."

"I know it," said Virgil.

"So don't get lost."

There was no chance of that. He was only going to the other side of the van. But as soon as he crossed the front and started down the driver's side, Virgil started thinking of the forest all around him. It didn't matter that his brother and sister were so close that he could hear their voices clearly. As he got down on his knees and reached under the van, he felt a prickling on the back of his neck. He was sure that something was watching from the trees.

"The thing came up behind him."

"Tore off his head."

It was embarrassing to be almost twelve years old and afraid of the dark. But Virgil couldn't help it. He had always been that way, afraid to go down to the basement at night, scared by the sounds of the house. *Blood in the River* had given him fears he had never known before. With his face turned toward the road, he groped round the curved end of the propane tank. Dried mud knocked loose by his fingers pattered onto the ground. The voices from the far side of the van gave him comfort. But the silence of the forest pricked at his mind.

"It watched them from the darkness, silent as the trees."

His arm brushed against something hard and springy. He'd found what he was looking for—the drain hose from the wastewater tank. But it swung away as he touched it, and he had to feel his way back to find it again. Then he walked his fingers down to the little tap at the end of the hose and slowly turned it open.

He was hoping for a trickle of water. But it came out of the hose in a warm rush, spilling over his hand and onto the road. It coated his fingers with a greasy slime that reeked of onions, soap, and spat-out toothpaste. He hurried to close the valve, then wiped his hand in the gravel.

When he stood up, Virgil was smiling. For a moment he forgot all about the forest and its terrible creatures. He walked round the front of the van as though nothing could scare him, thinking only how happy the others would be.

"Guess what?" he said, as he stopped in front of them. "I found lots of water."

Joshua lifted his head. "Where?" he asked.

"In the waste tank," said Virgil. "We can drain it out and—"

"The *waste tank*?" Joshua looked disgusted. "We can't drink that!"

"We can if we—"

"It's disgusting," said Kaitlyn. "That's water that went down the sink. It's gross!"

"Just listen!" said Virgil.

He was so frustrated that his voice broke into a squeak, like the cry of a little bird. He knew how to make the water pure and clean; his mom had shown him how to do it.

"I'll build a distiller," he said.

Kaitlyn laughed. "Why don't you just build a cell-phone tower?"

"Or a helicopter," said Joshua.

"It's not like that!" Virgil flapped his hands. "We've got everything we need in the van. It's easy."

Joshua didn't seem at all convinced, but he shrugged and said, "Well, okay, Virg. If you think you can do it, go ahead. Can we help you somehow?"

"You could take the water out of the tank," said Virgil.

"I'll get the bucket," said Kaitlyn.

Virgil turned on the interior lights and gathered anything that might be useful. He laid everything out on the counter: a ball of string, a cork, a rubber band. In the back of the silverware drawer he found a plastic box with another of his mother's labels: "Dad's tool kit." When he opened it, Virgil laughed. Inside was only one thing: half a roll of gray duct tape. He found a first-aid kit in the glove box, but nothing inside that he could use. He took an old Coke bottle from a cupboard, a funnel from under the seat. Then, without thinking, he reached up to the shelf and found the little wooden box with its brass engraving: Laura Pepper.

He touched the shiny tag, feeling the tiny loops of the letters scratched into the metal. In his mind he saw his mother's face, her blue eyes bright with happiness. He heard her voice, laughing, and it was easy to think that the box held her soul, or whatever he wanted to call it. But there were only ashes inside, just a few handfuls of potassium, sodium, and calcium phosphates. Ashes couldn't think; they couldn't feel. His mother's memories and hopes were not sealed in the box. It made no sense that Virgil could imagine her with him, right there in the van. But he did. He could feel her watching him, trying to help him.

In his mind he heard her voice, an echo from a year before, and he remembered sitting in her classroom on a busy morning. He could see the table where she'd arranged the same sort of things he had piled on Rusty's counter.

– – –

His mom is standing at the table, a magician about to transform an ordinary object into something amazing. "Everyone come up and see this," she says.

With a squealing of chairs, a thumping of desks, the kids

stand up all at once. The eager ones push to the front while others hang back, and one tall boy stands behind everyone else, swinging his head back and forth to see between them. Not believing that a coffeepot and a roll of duct tape could possibly save their lives, the kids whisper and laugh. They crack stupid jokes.

Virgil's mom waits for everyone to be quiet. She's so patient she might stand there forever, smiling at even the dumbest jokes.

Finally, she starts to talk. "Imagine there's been a disaster," she says. "An earthquake has leveled half the city. Your taps have gone dry, and the water's contaminated. What are you going to do?

Somebody says, "Buy bottled water."

"Okay, that's one solution," Virgil's mother tells the class. "But everybody's going to be looking for bottled water, and any stores that are open will be sold out before you can get there. Well, remember the rule of three that we talked about? You can't live without water, so you collect it from the puddles and the gutters. Now you have a real dilemma. If you don't drink the water, you'll die of thirst. But if you do, you'll get dysentery. Maybe even cholera. It happens all over the world. More people die after a disaster than during it."

She sweeps her hands above the table, palms up, showing off her bits of pipe, her rubber bands, and twist ties. "Well, I'm going to show you how you can drink any water you can find. You can drink from a swamp if you want to. Even from a septic tank."

The kids groan and make disgusted faces. Logan, the class clown, sticks his finger in his mouth and pretends to throw up.

"Sounds disgusting, doesn't it?" says Mom. "But it's perfectly safe. All you need is a way to boil the water, and a way to catch the steam."

She can inspire anybody. Even Logan. He pushes his way to the table and stands right beside her, as though he's itching to go home and drink from his septic tank.

She takes a bit of copper pipe from her pile of things and jams it into the coffeepot's narrow spout.

"What's that for?" asks Logan.

"It's going to cool the steam," she says. "You'll see in a minute. Copper works best, but almost anything will do."

– – –

Virgil held the box of ashes like a genie's lamp, wishing his mother would suddenly appear to help him.

But Joshua came instead, the yellow bucket glowing in the darkness. "We got at least three gallons," he said. "It smells rotten."

Virgil tried to slip the box back on the shelf before Joshua could see it. But he wasn't fast enough.

"What are you doing with that?" asked Joshua. "Were you talking to it, Virg?"

Embarrassed, Virgil lied. "No."

"I do that sometimes. It feels good." Joshua put the bucket down on the road. The plastic sides warped as water slopped inside, spilling over the edge. "I heard Dad talking to it last night."

He stepped up into Rusty and reached out for the box.

The lamplight flashed on the hinges as Virgil put it into his hands.

"I started thinking she's trapped in here," said Joshua. "I thought when we open the box it will be like letting her out. But then I felt sad because she's going to be so alone out there at Little Lost Lake. All those nights with no one around. All winter in the snow. But that's just crazy, isn't it?"

"I don't know," said Virgil.

"There's an expression in Spanish, that if you die dreaming you die happily. But that's not right. Mom had so many things she wanted to do. How could she be happy?"

Virgil couldn't think of anything to say. Beside him, Joshua dusted the box with his shirt and put it back on the shelf. When he turned around, he stared at the things that Virgil had set out on the seat. "Is this really going to work?" he asked.

Virgil blushed. "I think so. But I need some pipe."

"What sort?"

"It doesn't matter. Copper would be best."

"What about the drain hose we used to empty the tank?"

"That's too short," said Virgil.

"Okay, I'll look." Joshua smiled at Virgil. It was forced, not really a smile at all. Then he stooped through the door and went away, and soon Virgil could hear him clattering around at the back of the van. Virgil searched again through all the places he'd searched before. In the cupboard under the sink he saw the plastic hose that led from the pump to the tap. It was more than two feet long, but no matter how hard he pulled it wouldn't come loose.

"Hey, Josh!" he shouted. "Can I cut the hose to the sink?"

His brother's voice seemed to come up through the floor. "Just do whatever you want. It doesn't matter."

Virgil grabbed the bread knife from the silverware drawer and hacked through the hose. He felt awful doing it, as though he was cutting out the veins of the poor old van. But half an hour later, his distiller was finished.

Even he thought it looked pathetic, as useless as the crazy contraptions he'd made out of Legos and cardboard and string. When Kaitlyn saw it she laughed out loud. But Joshua said it looked "kinda cool." He tipped his head from side to side and studied it from every angle. "How does it work?" he asked.

"The water boils in the coffeepot and condenses in the pipe," said Virgil. Like a mad scientist with a strange machine, he pointed out each part as he traced the water through his system. The cork was jammed into the kettle's mouth. The hose was pushed into a hole that he'd bored through the cork with the pencil. It looped up toward the window and down into the Coke bottle. "Any steam that escapes gets captured by the ladle," he said. It was lashed to the kettle's handle with its bowl suspended upside down above the cork. One end of a straw was wedged into the ladle, and the other into a funnel that stood up in the plastic box. "The steam runs down the straw and through the funnel."

Joshua nodded. "What does the bungee do?"

"It just holds it all together."

Kaitlyn snickered.

"So let's fire it up," said Joshua.

The water had sat in the waste tank for more than a year, ever since the last trip to Little Lost Lake, and it had the same stink as rotted cheese. As Virgil scooped it out of the bucket with his drinking glass, he thought how some of it must have been used by his mother. He imagined her bending over the sink, pumping the water up with her foot. She would have washed her face and brushed her teeth and boiled the hated broccoli in the water they were all about to drink—if the thing he'd made could really work.

Kaitlyn put her hand over her mouth and nose. "You're not going to poison us, are you?" she asked.

"I don't think so," said Virgil.

When the coffeepot was full, he turned on the burner and lit the gas. Yellow flames curled up around it, and a few drops of spilled water sizzled on the metal. The three Peppers watched without talking, all crowded together in the little space below the pop-up roof. Inside the coffeepot, the water began to bubble.

Steam oozed out through the cork and wafted up into the upside-down bowl of the ladle. Through the greenish glass of the Coke bottle, Virgil saw a bead of water appear at the end of the hose. It grew slowly bigger, then broke loose and fell into the bottle. Another followed, and then another, and soon a tiny stream was trickling from the hose.

"It's working!" said Kaitlyn. She nudged Virgil with her elbow. "You did it, Virg. You really did it."

Joshua leaned on his elbows and grinned. "*Estupendo!*" he said.

Virgil didn't know what that meant, but it didn't matter. He had never felt prouder than he did just then.

They boiled the pot dry and filled it again. The burning propane made its own water, condensing so thickly on the windows that it dribbled down the glass. Virgil scraped it off with the vindow-viper and collected that as well.

By dribbles and drips, the Coke bottle slowly filled. Ice-clear water rose through the narrow waist of the bottle, over its shoulders, into the neck. Virgil emptied it out into a jar and started filling it again. But it was barely half full when the stove started spluttering. The flames turned from blue to yellow and shrank to tiny fingers. Then, with a *pop*, they vanished altogether.

"Well, that's it," said Joshua. "We're out of propane."

As the flame went out, the night closed in around the van. Inside, Rusty's lights made everything yellow and dim. Outside, it was so dark that Virgil couldn't even see the trees at the side of the road. He remembered his mother's expression:

Black as a witch's hat.

8

The Wicked One

Forest fires never sleep. Though sunset cooled the air, the Avalanche Fire kept growing. It spread across the mountain at half a mile an hour, climbing slowly toward the summit.

A hundred feet above it stood a rocky bluff twice the height of the tallest trees. A sheer cliff of gray rock so remote that it had been climbed only three times, it was known by mountaineers as El Malvado, "The Wicked One." It formed a natural break that contained the fire on the lower part of the mountain.

The night wind helped as well. It blew downhill, holding back the fire. The valley had become a lake of swirling smoke five hundred feet deep.

9

Screaming in the Night

"Can we light a fire?" asked Virgil. "We could set up the distiller and make more water."

"Sure," said Kaitlyn.

But Joshua didn't like that idea. "What if we burn down the forest?"

"You sound just like Dad," said Kaitlyn with a bright laugh. "A little fire's not going to hurt anything. Mom would have one going by now."

That was certainly true. Their mom had loved her campfires, even in the rain. Every night at Little Lost Lake she had sat mesmerized by flames that danced inside a circle of stones. She had said once that fire was the first pet that humans ever made. "We captured it from the wild," she'd said, "when we were still living in caves. We tamed it and fed it. We made it ours."

"I think we need one tonight," said Kaitlyn. "It will keep the dark away."

That made the night sound dangerous to Virgil, a wild thing that would attack them if they couldn't hold it back. He found a dark forest ten times more frightening than a dark house. At Little Lost Lake, he had never wandered far from Rusty after the sun went down, certain that he would go crazy if he ever got lost in the nighttime forest.

Kaitlyn gathered wood along the road. In the middle of the gravel pit, thirty feet from Rusty, she made a pile of twigs and tiny branches that looked like a game of pick-up sticks. She lit the fire with the old BIC lighter they'd carried from state to state for almost three years. Her fire was barely bigger than a dinner plate, but Virgil set up his distiller beside it, propping the coffeepot on a pyramid of stones.

It worked, but not for long. First the hose began to melt. Then the kettle tipped over, spilling water into the fire, almost drowning the little flames.

Joshua said, "Give it up, Virg. We've got enough water for tomorrow. Let's just sit for a while."

It was a warm night, and the smoke from the fire chased the bugs away. With his brother on one side and his sister on the other, Virgil felt safe—even happy. They sat silently, watching the flames, until a rustling sound from the edge of the road made them all turn their heads at once.

"What was that?" asked Kaitlyn.

A mouse scurried out of the darkness. Two more came behind it, and they crossed the road in timid little dashes, stopping halfway across to lift their heads and twitch their noses before hurrying on.

"Three blind mice, see how they run," said Joshua.

Virgil laughed. He leaned back on the gravel with his hands behind his head and stared up at the stars. He liked to watch for satellites and saw one right away, a white dot racing across the Big Dipper. He tried to imagine what the tiny fire on the Boneyard would look like from there. It would be a single dot of light in the endless blackness of the valley of the Bigfoot, as insignificant as a single pixel on a giant IMAX screen. It would be exactly the same as what he was seeing as he watched the satellite cross the void between the stars. But to him, right beside it, the fire seemed powerful. It threw out a circle of light that fluttered and pulsed at the edges, as the darkness tried to force its way in.

A barred owl hooted its wondering, plaintive cry: *Who looks for you? Who looks for you?*

"Let's tell ghost stories," said Kaitlyn.

Joshua said, "Sure."

But Virgil cried, "No! Let's tell funny stories."

"I know one," said Joshua. He leaned back from the fire, stretched out his legs, and began an old story—about the day when both Kaitlyn and Virgil had fallen into an open septic tank. It made them laugh as though they hadn't heard it a hundred times, and when it was finished, Virgil said to tell another. Josh did. He told story after story, all the favorites that he'd learned from their mom and dad. There were ones about Kaitlyn and ones about Virgil, ones about their crazy uncle Birdy. Virgil kept poking the fire to send sparks whirling away into the dark. With that he made the circle stronger, and they all felt happy inside it.

Until an hour before midnight.

The first scream came out of the forest then, short and piercing. It made them turn all at once toward the sound, and then all at once toward one another. Their faces shone orange in the firelight; their voices fell to whispers.

"What was that?" asked Virgil.

"I don't know," said Joshua. "Maybe a squirrel."

"A squirrel?" Kaitlyn laughed a crazy sort of laugh. "I never heard a squirrel make a sound like that."

"Let's go sit in the van," said Virgil.

"Just a minute," said Kaitlyn. She put more wood on the fire, stretching the circle of light into the forest. Then they sat and waited, barely breathing.

Virgil thought of the men in Kaitlyn's book, hearing a howling that none of them had ever heard before. Their story hadn't ended with the creature tearing off their heads. It had gotten even scarier. *"On moonlit nights their ghosts have been seen in the forest, searching blindly for their own heads."*

The second scream was louder. Shrill and startling, it made Virgil jump.

"Oh, Josh," whispered Kaitlyn. "That sounds like a woman. She's getting murdered or something."

"No one's getting murdered," said Joshua. But his voice was too shaky to sound convincing. "I think mountain lions sound like that."

He's only guessing, Virgil thought. He doesn't know about mountain lions.

But something was out there, and Virgil listened for the crack of a twig or the rustle of leaves that would mean it was moving toward them. He felt his nerves twisting into little knots like the rubber band on a toy airplane.

Joshua took his phone from his pocket. He swiped the screen, turned on the flashlight, and tried to light up the forest around them. But it made gruesome shadows among the trees and didn't help at all.

"We should sit in the van," said Virgil again, almost desperate now.

"Yes, why don't you do that?" asked Kaitlyn. "Go sit in the van and lock the door."

But Virgil didn't move. It was too far to go on his own, across the little clearing. It was too dark, the trees too close around him. The thing would catch him before he was half-way to the van.

Joshua poked at the fire. He stirred up a cloud of sparks that lit his face with a ghastly gruesome light. The circle grew bigger, then shrank again as the flames cowered down among the bits of wood. Virgil stared straight into the flames, not wanting to see what was out there, waiting with his hands squeezed tightly into fists.

But nothing bounded from the dark to kill them. Nothing screamed or shrieked or made any sound at all.

In the fire a branch exploded, flinging red embers across the gravel pit. The sound made them all start, and then laugh nervously. Joshua used a stick to scrape the shattered embers into a little heap, which pulsed in the dark like a beating heart.

"Well, I guess it's gone," he said. "Whatever it was."

Virgil thought, No, it hasn't gone. It's right there. It's just outside the circle.

But Joshua shut off his light, tossed his stick into the fire, and said, "Let's go to bed now."

"You guys go ahead," said Kaitlyn. "I'll wait till the fire goes out."

"Okay, I'll wait with you," said Joshua.

Virgil was already on his feet, but he sat right back down again. "I'll wait too," he said.

"Oh, Virg." Kaitlyn sighed and touched his arm. "We'll be right here. We're just twenty feet away."

It was at least thirty feet, but Virgil didn't say so. "I want to hear another story," he said. "Please."

He would never get to sleep if those screams were the last things he heard before bed. They would ring in his ears all night long.

"All right, one more," said Joshua.

"Tell the bicycle story," said Virgil.

Joshua groaned. "I already told it."

"I know," said Virgil. "I love that story."

So Joshua began it all over again. "When Dad and Birdy were little kids, they lived at the top of a hill."

He told the story just the way their father had always told it, almost word for word. "It was a very long hill, and the road turned back and forth, and down at the bottom was a swamp."

Virgil knew the story so well that his mind went straight to the ending. He thought about his dad and Uncle Birdy coated in mud, about his granddad hosing them down and then hanging them on the clothesline with the laundry. Thinking about it made him laugh before Joshua was even halfway into the story. Feeling cozy and happy, he wriggled up beside the fire.

And the screaming started again.

Joshua turned his head and gazed into the darkness as though he was watching a ghost.

Embers popped in the fire with a sound that seemed too loud. They made little bursts of light that pushed back the dark for a moment or two. Virgil wondered if they might push it back so far that he would see something standing just beyond the circle's edge, something huge and shaggy.

There was another scream. Joshua turned his head toward the forest. "You're right," he said. "It sounds like a woman."

"You should go look," said Kaitlyn.

"No!" said Virgil. "Stay here."

But Kaitlyn said, "Please, Josh. You're probably right; it's just an animal. But we have to know for sure."

Joshua got up from the fire. It was obvious that he didn't want to go. He stood with his hands hanging down at his sides, still peering into the forest. A bat fluttered through the air above him and went wheeling away into the darkness.

"You should stay here with Virgil, and I'll go look," said Kaitlyn. "Girls see better in the dark."

Virgil had no idea if that was true. He thought she was only saying it to make Joshua feel better.

It seemed that Joshua thought that too. "No, I'm going," he said. Then he reached down and pulled from the fire the same stick he'd put into it just a short while before. Little waggling fingers of flames clung to the tip.

Holding it high, he led the way to the van. He ushered Virgil and Kaitlyn inside, then grabbed the door by the handle to slide it shut.

But Kaitlyn blocked it with her foot. "Leave it open," she said.

Joshua turned around and took a step away. His hands were shaking so badly that the flames swooped through the air on the end of the stick. But he took another step, and then another, and suddenly he was striding away across the gravel pit, through the campfire's circle of light. As he reached the edge and climbed up to the forest, it seemed that he took a part of the circle along with him. But it was pale and fluttery, and it grew fainter as each little finger let go. Soon all he carried was a red glow, an eye that winked in the darkness as he passed behind the trees. It vanished, reappeared, then vanished again.

Virgil heard Joshua calling out, "Hello?" But only once, and then there was nothing. He moved his head up and down, back and forth, trying to see where his brother had gone. "Can you see him, Kait?"

"No." She stepped out onto the Boneyard.

"Don't go away!" cried Virgil.

"I'm not going anywhere," she said. "I just want to stand outside."

Virgil couldn't see much more than the starry sky and

the hints of things around him: the pale strip of the Boneyard, the bushes at the roadside, the trees behind them. But there was no red eye moving through the forest, no sign of his brother.

Kaitlyn called out, though not very loudly, "Josh?"

There was no answer.

"Joshua?"

Virgil thought how easy it would be to get lost in the darkness. The fire seemed too small to guide his brother back.

"I'll turn on the lights," he said. He moved through the van, switching them on one by one, until the canvas tent glowed. Finally, he climbed into the driver's seat and turned on the high-beam headlights.

They lit up the Boneyard as far as the bend, glaring off the gravel. A cloud of moths flurried round the lamps, and their shadows wheeled across the road as big as owls. A raccoon stood frozen in the middle of the road, looking back at Virgil with its eyes gleaming yellow. Then it hunched up its back and scuttled into the darkness.

Kaitlyn shouted again. "Josh!"

Virgil honked the horn. He pressed hard on the big, round button in the middle of the steering wheel. They had always laughed at the sound it made, a hollow hooting *beep*, but Virgil imagined his brother hearing it far away, lifting his head, trying to tell where it was coming from. *Beep! Beep!*

Virgil kept honking, and Kaitlyn kept shouting, and down by the bend in the road a white glow appeared in the forest. It slid between the trees and out to the road, and into the bright beams of Rusty's headlights stumbled Joshua, lighting his way with his iPhone. He turned it off as he walked quickly toward the van.

"Here comes Josh!" cried Virgil. He clambered down from Rusty's front seat and ran to meet their brother.

"Stay in the van!" shouted Joshua. Almost jogging down the road, he turned Virgil around without stopping and herded him back to the van, "Hurry," he said. "But don't run."

Kaitlyn was waiting there when they came up together. "What's going on?" she asked.

"Something's out there," said Joshua. "It was trying to get me."

"What is it?"

"I don't know." He pushed Virgil and Kaitlyn through the big door, climbed in behind them, and slammed it shut. "Turn out the lights," he said.

Virgil switched off the headlights, and Kaitlyn the lamps. She left only one of them burning, the little yellow light above the sink. With Virgil in the front, Kaitlyn and Joshua in the back, they looked through the windows into the dark.

"So what happened out there?" asked Kaitlyn.

"Well, I didn't get very far," said Joshua. "I was barely in among the trees. Then I got that feeling—you know—like someone's watching you?"

Virgil nodded. He knew that feeling well.

"I called out, but nobody answered," said Joshua.

"There was something nearby. I just knew it," said Joshua. "It might have been a person, or it might have been an animal; I just knew it was there. So I blew out the torch and waited for it to go away. But it didn't. I could hear it coming closer. It was moving through the bushes. It sounded like it was over here, and then over there, and then behind me."

"What do you think it was?" asked Virgil.

"I don't know."

"How big was it?"

"I didn't see it."

"But was it bigger than a bear?"

"Virgil! I didn't see it."

They were almost at code yellow. Kaitlyn said, "He wants to know if it was Sasquatch."

Joshua laughed. "Seriously? A Sasquatch?"

"It's possible!" cried Virgil.

"No, it's not," said Joshua.

"How do you know?"

"Because there's no such thing."

"Dead parrot," said Virgil.

"Grow up," said Joshua.

"Don't tell me to grow up," said Virgil. "Mom used to say that." Whenever someone in her class gave an answer like Joshua's, she would say, "That's a dead parrot. It doesn't tell me anything."

"So what happened next?" asked Kaitlyn. "What did you do?"

"I backed away," said Joshua. "Slowly. Like they tell you to do if you meet a bear. Whatever it was, it kept coming after me. I couldn't see a thing, but I heard it. It was hunting me."

"You think it's still out there?" asked Virgil.

"Probably," said Joshua.

"Do you think it will try to get in?"

"No, Virg," said Kaitlyn, in her calming voice. "We're safe in here. Whatever's out there, it will be gone by the morning."

For the first time in seven years, Joshua slept inside the van. He had a little orange pup tent stuffed in the bag under the back seat, but he didn't set it up that night. Instead, he used the big bed above the engine compartment, his parents' place. Kaitlyn climbed into her old spot on the platform she called "the top shelf," high under the canvas roof. Virgil had thought he'd be moving up there at last, with Joshua in his tent and Kaitlyn on the big bed. But he ended up on the floor where he'd always slept, with his head between the front seats.

Just as before, every place in the van was full. But everything was different. They didn't tell silly jokes before settling down to sleep. They didn't talk about the things they would do in the morning. Now there was only the whining of the mosquitoes. Virgil missed his mother's laugh.

On the big bed, Joshua started snoring. From the forest came that strange cry of a barred owl. *Who looks for you? Who looks for you?*

DAY TWO

10

The Beast

At dawn, the Cessna returned to the Avalanche Fire. The pilot and his spotter found a line of flames at the base of the cliffs. As though looking for a way around them, the fire was spreading in both directions.

Down the mountain and along the valley, five hundred acres of forest were burning. But if the fire worked its way around El Malvado there'd be nothing to keep it from growing. It would run up the mountain and over the ridge to the neighboring valley of the Bigfoot River. If it jumped El Malvado, there would be no way to stop it.

Of the six other fires lit by the lightning storm, three had been put out. A hotshot crew returning from one of them was sent straight back out again—to stop the Avalanche Fire.

Dropped in by helicopter, they set to work with chain saws and Pulaskis, with scrapers and drip torches. A mile ahead of the fire's leading edge, they cut a break across its path. They knocked down trees and scraped the earth away to dig a trench that the fire could not cross. Then they set fire to the forest, trying to burn up the fuel that the fire needed to feed itself.

At the same time, another crew was dropped off at the end of a logging road fifteen miles away. With forty pounds of equipment on their backs, the men started hiking toward the fire. They could see the flames rising over the trees and the smoke rolling down the valley, and they gave their own name to the fire.

They called it "the Beast."

11

Just Like Uncle Birdy

Virgil was the last to fall asleep and the last to wake in the morning. On his back on the floor, he looked up through the windshield at a clear sky that shimmered with heat. He could hear Kaitlyn and Joshua talking outside.

"We can't just sit here," she said. "I think we should start walking back to the highway."

"Thirty-four miles? In this heat?" Joshua made a noise that was half-groan and half-grunt. "Virgil couldn't make it that far."

"Then why not go to Trickleback Creek?"

"We're not walking all that way for a drink of water," said Joshua. "That's worse than staying here."

"Then we don't come back," she said. "We wait at the creek till someone comes by."

Joshua shook his head. "It's going to be dried up. Virgil's right about that."

"I could take the bucket and—"

"No." Joshua sounded very firm, as though nothing would change his mind. "We have to stick together. No matter what."

For another few minutes Virgil stayed where he was. Then he pretended to wake, with a lot of noise and dramatic groans as he got out of his sleeping bag. By the time he joined the others outside, the day was already hotter than the one before. They shared half of the second can of soup, then settled down to wait for help to come. Virgil dragged his sleeping bag outside and stretched out in the shade beside Rusty. Kaitlyn didn't go back to her place below the alder tree, preferring instead to sit with Joshua at the edge of the gravel pit. Like a pride of lions they lay sluggish in the heat, only Joshua ever moving. Now and then he raised his head and looked down the road, as though watching for a herd of gazelles to come bounding along.

Nobody mentioned food or water as the time went slowly by. Nobody talked at all. Virgil watched a grasshopper bounce along the road on rattling wings, and then an ant making its way through the gravel. As a tiny tank would move through a field of boulders, it stopped and started, backed and turned. He piled pebbles in its way and watched it scurry around them, then rolled on his side as it disappeared under the van.

The puddle of oil and antifreeze had dried to a black stain. The ant went straight across it and vanished in the shadows.

From where he was, stretched out on the road, Virgil

could see the tangle of pipes and hoses. In his head he heard the gruff voice of his uncle Birdy. "If a guy can build it, I can fix it."

Uncle Birdy didn't know any words that had more than two syllables. He had never been more than a hundred miles from his house. He had a big barrel of a body and enormous hands turned black by oil and dirt, and Virgil thought of him as a genius. He loved to watch his uncle at work at the big wooden bench in a garage crowded with bits and pieces of everything ever made. With his glasses balanced on the very tip of his nose, Uncle Birdy would lean back his head and mutter away under his breath as he fiddled with gears and bolts. He would never sit still if there was a broken-down van to be fixed. Virgil moved to the back of the van to get a better look at the engine. Joshua shouted at him, "What are you doing, Virg?"

"Nothing," said Virgil. "Just looking."

"It would be better if you stayed away from there."

"I might be able to fix it."

"Nobody can fix it," said Joshua.

"But Uncle Birdy says—"

"Oh, forget Uncle Birdy!" Joshua got up and walked toward Virgil. "If Uncle Birdy is such a mechanical genius, why is his garage full of junk that he can't put back together?"

"They're works in progress," said Virgil, quoting his uncle.

"Except nothing works and nothing progresses." Joshua stopped at Rusty's open doorway. "You know more than Uncle Birdy about a lot of things. He couldn't have done what you did with the water."

That made Virgil feel sorry for his uncle but happy for himself. He'd had no idea that his brother felt that way.

"But Rusty's dead," said Joshua. "Forget about fixing it." He pulled himself up into the van and brought out the Coke bottle and a drinking glass. He gave Virgil the first small drink, and Kaitlyn exactly the same amount. But for himself, he poured out barely enough to cover the bottom of the glass.

It was noon, the sun nearly right overhead. Virgil tried to hold the water in his mouth for as long as he could, but his tongue seemed to soak it up. He felt just as thirsty as he'd been before.

Joshua put the glass and the bottle back in the van. When he came out again, he smiled at Virgil. But it was an awful smile that looked more worried than happy.

"Everything's going to work out," he said, and patted Virgil on the shoulder. "We'll be okay. I promise."

Virgil nodded, but he didn't believe it. You can't promise that, he thought. You can say it, but it doesn't mean anything.

Virgil moved back to his old place in the van's open doorway. The flies followed him, zooming round his head. Tired of swatting them away, he huddled into a little ball and tried to ignore them.

Just like his uncle Birdy, he couldn't forget about the van. He imagined himself solving the problem, then climbing into the driver's seat to start the engine. In his mind he heard it turn over, sputter, and start. He heard Joshua saying, "*Ay caramba*, that's amazing!" and he saw Kaitlyn dancing around, singing, "He did it! He did it!" He saw himself driving down the road with Kaitlyn and Joshua in the back seat, the engine roaring behind them. It didn't matter that he'd never driven a car. Video games had taught him everything. He could leap canyons and outrun police cars. The Boneyard would be easy.

The story took over his mind completely. Instead of the forest and the gravel pit, Virgil was looking at the Boneyard through Rusty's windshield, seeing it unwinding in front of him as he sped through the forest. He heard the engine's throbbing roar and the gravel crunching under the wheels. Then another sound—a distant sound—made the movie in his head come to a sudden end.

He sat up straight. He turned his head and listened, and there it was again, a hum and flutter of machines.

"What's that noise?" he asked.

The others sat up in the grass. "I don't hear anything," said Kaitlyn.

"Listen," said Virgil.

They sat so still that they might have been dead. Kaitlyn asked, "What do you think you heard?"

And Joshua said, "Shhh! I hear it too."

Far in the distance, the sound rose and fell. It stopped altogether and started again. A frantic sort of noise, it reminded Virgil of a bee trapped in a jar.

"What is that?" asked Joshua. He stood up and looked toward the sound. There was nothing to see but the trees, and—between their tops—the gray-green summit of Headless Mountain. "I think it might be motorcycles."

"I think it's chain saws," said Virgil.

"Or helicopters," added Kaitlyn.

Joshua shook his head. "No, it's motorcycles. And it's coming from there." He pointed through the trees. "From Headless Mountain."

"But there's no road on the mountain," said Virgil.

"They're dirt bikes. They're probably riding up the mountain. They can't be more than six or seven miles away."

Virgil didn't believe it. To him, the sound was much more distant than that—maybe an echo from the other end of the valley, or even from the far side of the mountain.

"If it's only six miles we should start walking," said Kaitlyn.

But Joshua said, "Not yet."

"Why?"

"I still think somebody's going to drive by. If not, we'll leave in the morning when it's cooler."

Nobody drove by. And the day grew hotter and hotter, until Virgil was sure he could smell Rusty's tires melting in the sun. Every now and then a leaf fluttered down from one of the alder trees, though there wasn't a breath of wind to knock them loose. Like dead butterflies, they fell in silent, tumbling circles.

Late in the afternoon, the distant sounds became clearer than ever. Both Kaitlyn and Joshua kept looking toward Headless Mountain, trying to peer through the forest. Even Virgil began to believe the sounds were coming closer, and he wished he could see over the tops of the trees.

And that thought was both the beginning of everything and the end of everything.

12

Climbing the Tree

Virgil walked along the road, looking for a tree that would be easy to climb. Fifty yards from the van he found it, an old alder with so many branches that it looked like Jack's magic beanstalk rising into the sky. If he could jump high enough to reach the first branch, the rest would be easy.

Just leaving the road seemed the hardest part of all. There had been no sign of the thing that had screamed in the night, the thing that had hunted Joshua. But Virgil didn't believe it had gone away. In *Blood in the River*, the Sasquatches had waited three days before suddenly attacking a man in his cabin.

What would he do if one caught him climbing the tree? It was too far from the van for any chance to run back. Virgil saw himself scrambling up the tree, hauling himself from branch to branch, higher and higher, until he was clinging to twigs at the very top. The tree would be swaying back and forth, and he would hear the Sasquatch coming behind him, the branches snapping under its weight. The leaves would fall away in clouds, and through them he would see the Sasquatch, huge and shaggy, coming hand over fist up the tree.

Maybe Kaitlyn should climb it.

The idea flashed into Virgil's mind. She had been climbing trees since she was five years old; it would be nothing to her to climb this one. Every week she practiced on a fifty-foot wall in the gym, clinging by her toes and fingers to bits of plastic no bigger than berries. But climbing the tree was his idea, and he wanted to be the one to do it. So he took a long look into the forest and ran to the foot of the tree.

The first branch was higher than he'd thought. When he jumped, his fingers only brushed against the bark. But he tried again, and then again, each time with a grunt as he launched himself from the ground.

It was Joshua who saw him jumping up and down, and Joshua who called up from the road. "Virgil, what are you doing now?"

"Climbing the tree," said Virgil. He peered over the bank to see both Joshua and Kaitlyn standing there.

"Why are you climbing a tree?" asked Kaitlyn.

"To look around," said Virgil. "I want to see the mountain."

Joshua nodded his head. "Yeah, okay. That's not a bad idea."

"Maybe I should climb it," said Kaitlyn.

"No." As he'd done a dozen times before, Virgil bent his knees and leaped from the ground. This time he got his hands right around the branch. But he wasn't strong enough to haul himself up, and he just dangled from the tree with his legs kicking.

Joshua laughed. Kaitlyn said, "Virg, just let me do it, please."

"No," said Virgil again. He swung his feet desperately, back and forth, higher and higher, until he finally hooked one over the branch. Then he hung there like a sloth, with his head tipped back, not knowing what to do next.

Kaitlyn came up from the road and stood beside him. Her head was level with his but upside down in his vision. "It's okay," she said. "Not everyone can climb trees."

She reached out to help him down. But Virgil just lowered his feet and dropped to the ground. Hanging head down had made him so dizzy that he took a staggering step and fell over. When he sat up, Kaitlyn was already high above him, climbing steadily up the tree.

Sun-dried leaves crackled as she pushed them apart. They broke loose and tumbled slowly down.

Virgil shouted from the grass. "Are you at the top?"

"Almost," she said.

"What do you see?"

"Not much."

Joshua leaned back and called up to her. "Do you see anyone on the mountain?"

"Are you kidding?" she said. "I can't even see the mountain."

Virgil had not chosen the tallest tree. Even at the top, Kaitlyn was far below the tips of the smallest pines. All she could see was the forest.

"I'm coming down," she said.

A shower of twigs and broken leaves rained onto Virgil. He covered his eyes and turned aside.

And so he didn't see Kaitlyn falling.

There was a crack as a branch split in two, a cry of surprise, and a crashing of sticks and leaves. Joshua roared, "Kait!"

She came down in a blur and landed with a thud, right in front of Virgil. Too surprised to move, he stood gaping at her with his mouth in a little round circle.

Kaitlyn lay in a heap, not moving.

Joshua came running up the slope and hurled himself down beside her. "Are you all right?" he asked.

"No." She kept her face toward the ground, but she couldn't hide her pain. It was in her voice, the way it quavered when she spoke. "I think I broke my ankle."

"Well, don't get up," said Joshua.

But of course she ignored him. She started moving her arms and her fingers, her wrists and knees, testing every bone and joint. She didn't even wince until she shifted her legs. Then she yelped.

"Oh, that doesn't look good," said Joshua.

Her left ankle looked bruised and swollen, bulging between the straps of her sandals. Virgil could hardly believe it had gotten so bad so quickly.

"Help me up," she said.

"I think you should keep lying down for a while," said Joshua.

"I want to see if I can put any weight on it."

They stood behind her, Joshua on one side and Virgil on the other. Joshua did most of the lifting, but Virgil tried to keep his sister balanced. She held her foot above the ground, the way a dog protects a sore paw, and limped between her brothers.

"How are you doing?" asked Joshua.

"It hurts pretty bad," she said.

Hearing that scared Virgil more than anything. He had seen his sister come home with broken teeth and bleeding fingers, with more stitches than Frankenstein's monster. But he'd never once heard her admit that something hurt.

Now, just a touch of her toe on the ground made her cry out.

Virgil imagined that he could see her ankle swelling. It was turning black and purple.

"This changes everything," said Joshua. "We have to find help right now."

"But she can't walk," said Virgil.

"I know that," said Joshua. "I have to go alone."

13

Like a Hive of Bees

Joshua got the bottle of Advil from the first-aid kit in Rusty's glove box. There were only four tablets, so he told Kaitlyn to make them last. Then he patted his pockets to make sure he had his cell phone, and he said, "Well, I guess I'll go now."

He wouldn't take any soup. He wouldn't take any water. "Kaitlyn's going to need it more than me," he said. "Anyway, I don't have far to go. Those people can't be more than five miles away."

"I think they're farther than that," said Virgil.

Joshua shook his head. "Just listen."

The sound was definitely louder than before. It swelled and shrank but was always there, droning like a hive of bees. Joshua had changed his mind about motorcycles, and now they all agreed. Somewhere on Headless Mountain, loggers were working with chain saws and helicopters.

"I should be there in two or three hours," said Joshua. "Who knows; maybe I'll get a cell-phone signal somewhere along the way."

As though he didn't really want to go at all, Joshua fussed with everything. He untied and retied his shoes three times, and when he was finally ready he stood in the middle of the Boneyard for another minute more. He asked both Virgil and Kaitlyn, "Are you sure you'll be all right?"

"Yes," said Kaitlyn.

"Do you think—?"

"I'm fifteen years old!" she shouted. "Just go, will you, Josh?"

"Okay." He held up his hands in that surrendering way that was just like their dad's. "With any luck, someone could be here before dark. But don't be scared if nobody comes. Lock yourselves in the van and wait until morning." He looked right at Virgil with a strange, forced smile. "Nothing to worry about, buddy."

Buddy. Whenever his brother used that word there was lots to worry about. But Virgil only nodded.

"Okay," said Joshua again. "*Adios, amigos*. I'll see you later."

He took a few steps down the road. Then he suddenly stopped and turned around, and without a word he climbed into the van and got the box of ashes.

"You're taking that with you?" asked Kaitlyn.

"No," he said. "I just want to make sure it's not left behind."

He held the box the way he would hold a football,

tucked tightly under his arm. "I might not be with them when they come to pick you up. Make sure you take this box. Okay?"

"Okay," said Kaitlyn.

"It's the most valuable thing we have."

"I know," said Kaitlyn.

"I'll set it right here." Joshua opened the passenger door and placed the box on the seat, where their mother had always sat. "You won't forget it. Right?"

"No, we won't forget it," said Kaitlyn.

As though he thought he might never do it again, Joshua touched the box one more time. His fingers pressed down on the polished wood and lingered there for a moment. Then he took them away, closed the door, and turned around.

"Look after each other," he said. "Remember: It's just one night. Tomorrow we'll all be home."

He walked down the road and didn't look back. But he held up his hand and waved. It was a comical wave, with his fingers waggling. "*Hasta la vista*," he said.

Virgil wanted to run after him, either to stop him from leaving or to go along with him. It didn't matter. He just didn't want to spend another night on the Boneyard without his big brother. But to run crying after him would be even worse. So Virgil just stood beside the van and watched him go. Fifty yards down the road, Joshua turned left and waded through the grass. He parted the bushes in front of him and disappeared down the hillside, into the forest.

For a little while longer, Virgil could hear him stepping

over sticks and branches. When those sounds faded away, he felt lonelier than ever.

"Hey, Virgil," said Kaitlyn. "You should find some firewood. We have to be ready before it gets dark."

He didn't like being bossed around, not even five minutes after their brother left. But he went off to fetch the wood, knowing she couldn't do it herself.

Along the roadside, Virgil gathered an armload of small branches and scraps of bark. As Kaitlyn had done the night before, he piled them in the clearing and went back to find more. The third time he passed her, Kaitlyn looked up. "Hey, I'm sorry," she said.

He stopped, then turned back. "For what?"

"For getting us stuck here," she told him. "For falling out of that tree."

Again, she seemed just like his mom. In pain but not complaining, ready to take the blame for anything at all. He said, "It's my fault."

Kaitlyn frowned. "How's it your fault?"

"'Cause I can't climb trees."

Virgil started picking tiny specks of bark from the front of his shirt. He was aware of Kaitlyn watching him, but didn't look at her.

"Oh, Virgil," she said. "It's amazing that you tried. You could have killed yourself, but you did it anyway. I would never have done that."

He picked off another bit of bark and flicked it from his fingers. "You can do anything."

"Like run fast and hit a ball?" she said. "Big deal. You're lucky. You're smart."

He knew she was trying to make him feel better. His mother had tried the same thing, telling him that the kids who bullied him now would be reading about him in the news someday because he'd done something fantastic. "And you know what?" she'd said. "They'll be telling everyone who'll listen, 'I used to know that guy; I went to school with Virgil Pepper.'" It was a nice thought, but he'd rather be strong and tough.

"I mean it, Virg," said Kaitlyn. "If we were in the Hunger Games or something, I bet you'd be the one who survived." Then she smiled. "Brains beat muscles any day."

She was quoting their mother. The memory of it took Virgil back in time.

– – –

They're just finishing dinner on a day in late December. Snow is falling outside, and in the corner stands the Christmas tree, hung with red lights and silver garlands. Joshua has taken his dessert into the living room. He's watching Die Hard *again.*

Mom picks the green cherries from her piece of Christmas cake and sets them aside. She hates the green cherries. She says, "Who do you think would win a fight: Bruce Willis or Stephen Hawking?"

The question comes so suddenly that it makes them laugh. But she asks it seriously, with a frown on her face, as though she's been puzzled for years.

Dad says, "There's no contest. Bruce could snap the guy in half."

"With one hand tied behind his back," adds Kaitlyn.

But Mom says, "I'm not sure. I think Stephen Hawking might win."

"How?" asks Kaitlyn.

"I'm not sure. He'd come up with something really clever. He'd set a trap or something."

Dad shrugs one shoulder. "It's possible."

"I'm sure of it," says Mom. "Brains beat muscles any day."

– – –

Virgil went away for one more load of firewood. He walked with his head held up, feeling proud of himself. As he passed behind Rusty, he wanted more than ever to fix the old van. As he had before, he imagined himself starting the engine and driving down the Boneyard. But now he saw his sister lying on the back seat, calling out to him faintly, "You're a winner, Virg."

On the side of the van that Kaitlyn couldn't see, Virgil lay down on the gravel. He squirmed underneath the engine and reached up to grab the hose that he'd thought was leaking. It felt hard and greasy, as thick as a baseball bat. When he pushed it sideways, a drop of antifreeze fell from the darkness and splashed on his cheek. Frantically, he wiped it off and smeared his fingers on his T-shirt, afraid that it would blind him if it got in his eyes. "That stuff's poisonous. It kills dogs." Virgil lay on his back on the gravel, staring up at a black smudge of hoses and metal.

With his eyes closed, he felt his way along the hose.

It was clamped to a plastic fitting, a sort of octopus head where three other hoses came together. As he wiggled and pushed them, another drop of antifreeze plopped onto the road.

He couldn't tell where it had come from. But the fitting was wet, oozing antifreeze when he pushed against it. Though he couldn't see a thing in the black tangle of rubber, Virgil was sure he'd found the leak. Now all he had to do was fix it.

"Figuring out what's wrong, that's half the battle," Uncle Birdy would say. "Yup, figurin's hard. Fixin's easy."

14

On the Mountain

The sky was turning pink as Joshua Pepper bashed his way toward Headless Mountain. What he'd thought would be an easy walk through the forest had become a struggle. He wrestled his way through tangled bushes, sometimes swimming over their tops with his hands and feet not even touching the ground.

The hordes of flies nearly drove him crazy. He swatted at them; he shouted at them. At one point, he just stood in one spot for nearly a minute, waving his arms and screaming. He had never felt more frustrated.

Wherever he turned, Joshua found an obstacle in front of him. A wall of thorns, a wind-fallen tree, a rocky bluff too high to climb—they made him turn around and find another route. He climbed up little outcrops and squirmed under jumbles of fallen trees. In the first hour, he traveled less than a mile. In the third, as he started moving steadily uphill, he was going even slower.

Every few minutes he stopped and bent down with his hands on his knees, gasping great breaths that hurt his lungs. He peered through the trees around him, hoping to glimpse the flat summit that he'd thought would guide him all the way. But he hadn't seen it since he first walked into the forest. Afraid he was going in the wrong direction, Joshua closed his eyes and listened. There was a woodpecker somewhere, tapping on a tree. And somewhere else, much farther away, someone was running a chain saw.

Joshua turned and plodded toward the sound, still certain that he was hearing loggers.

But he was wrong about that.

15

Flinging Flames

The hotshot crew hiked up Headless Mountain through wisps of thin smoke. In hard hats and aramid shirts, in leather gloves and tall boots, they looked like creatures from another world, invaders of the forest.

On a patch of level ground they stopped to build a helispot, first digging a fire line to protect them if the Beast went wild. With the blades of their Pulaskis clanging off hidden stones, they chopped through the forest floor.

Their chain saws whined and growled as they knocked down trees to make the platform for the helicopters.

Three miles away, the fire was raging below El Malvado. Giant flames hurled themselves at the cliffs as though storming the walls of a castle. Again, it seemed as though the fire had a thinking mind and a plan to conquer the mountain.

But with a crew on the leading edge and another below it, the Beast seemed well contained. A caged animal, it could only prowl back and forth behind its bars. When it consumed the forest in its cage, it would wither away and die.

16

A Flock of Crows

With the setting of the sun, the sky turned red and pink. The colors were vivid, as bright as neon lights, the sort of sunset that would have made his mother stop whatever she was doing to watch it. Nothing was too important, she used to say, that you couldn't stop to watch the sunset.

Virgil remembered sitting beside her on the low bluff above Little Lost Lake, just the two of them watching the sun go down.

"Why is it so red?" he asks.

They've spent an hour swimming in the lake, and now they've climbed up onto the rocky knoll. Virgil is wearing his towel as a cape, but he's so cold that he shivers in little spasms. His toes, wrinkled by the water, look like puffy mushrooms.

"Sunlight is made of seven colors," she tells him. "They get separated as the particles of light come through the atmosphere and bounce off the air molecules. The shorter their wavelength, the more easily they're scattered. Blue has a short wavelength, and red has the longest. When the sun is low, at sunrise and sunset, the light has to pass through more of the atmosphere, so there's more time for the colors to scatter. One by one they bounce away, until only the red light is left to reach us."

Virgil stares at his toes and tries to figure that out. "Then why isn't the blue light scattered in the daytime?"

"Well, it is," she says. "That's why the sky looks blue. Because blue light is scattered all over the place."

He loves that she talks to him as though he's an adult. But sometimes it makes his head hurt.

Down below them, a loon paddles alone across the lake. A gentle breeze ripples the water and makes Virgil shiver.

"You're cold," says Mom.

"I'm okay."

She pulls him sideways and hugs him. She rubs the goose bumps from his arms. "You know what I like to think about?"

"What?"

"Somewhere off to the west—thousands of miles away—it's noon right now. People are looking straight up at a white sun in a blue sky. They're seeing the very same molecules of air that we're seeing, but to them the sky looks completely different."

He leans against her. His teeth have begun to chatter, but he wants to stay and talk.

"I love that idea," she says. "The world isn't necessarily the

way we see it, and what we think is real might be an illusion. Maybe that's true for the big, important things too."

– – –

"Look up!" said Kaitlyn. A few yards away, she was pointing up at the sky.

A flock of crows was passing over the gravel pit. In a glance, Virgil saw thirty or forty, and then thirty more. They flew in ragged bunches, little wind-whipped clouds of crows, more than he'd ever seen at one time. Black shapes on the red sky, they came from the north, from Headless Mountain, and the only sound was an airy *whoosh* from their wings.

He wondered where they were going, and why. They seemed ominous, unsettling in their silence, driving along with their wings beating quickly. He remembered something his father had told him. A bunch of crows is called a murder.

Behind them came an eagle, its huge wings rippling. And behind the eagle came a pair of gulls, and next a racing falcon, and then a storm of little songbirds.

Kaitlyn watched them pass as she lay on her back on the sleeping bag. "What's going on?" she asked.

"I don't know," he said. And then, shyly, "Do you think it's 'cause of Mom?"

"'Cause of Mom? What do you mean?"

"I dunno." Virgil felt embarrassed, afraid that Kaitlyn

would laugh at him. "Remember how she used to feed the birds? How they gathered round her, from all over the place, and ate right out of her hand? Maybe it's like they're . . . like they're kind of thanking her. I don't know."

To his surprise, Kaitlyn didn't laugh. She didn't say she believed him, but that was okay. Even Virgil found it doubtful that birds could honor his mom with a flyby. But he couldn't think of any other reason why all the birds in the valley would suddenly be flying overhead.

When the sky was so dark that he couldn't see a thing, Virgil still heard the whistle of feathers and wings.

17

Only Silence

On top of the dead fire from the night before, Kaitlyn built a new one from the wood that Virgil had gathered. She did it lying down, stretched out in a mermaid's pose, with her long hair trailing on the ground.

"Half this stuff is rotten," she said as she sorted through the branches. She pulled out sticks that were hairy with moss, and twigs that were covered with mushrooms. Only the dry, dead wood went into her little pyramid.

Virgil sat beside her. He picked up one of her thrown-away sticks and started peeling off the bark. "Where do you think Josh is right now?" he asked.

"I was wondering that too," said Kaitlyn.

"Do you think he met up with anyone?"

"Well, I doubt it," she said. "Or they'd be here by now."

"Do you think he'll walk all night?"

"No," she said. "He'll have to sleep."

From her pile of firewood, Kaitlyn pulled out a stick so rotten that it crawled with grubs. They bubbled from the wood, squirming on top of one another. The writhing mass of them made Virgil feel squeamish, but Kaitlyn just tossed the stick aside and picked up another one, talking all the time.

"He's probably sleeping right now. Or trying to." She used a twig to push hair from her eyes, then put it on her pyramid. "He might be up on top of the mountain."

Virgil tried to picture his brother curled up all alone on the summit of Headless Mountain. He saw him first as though he was sitting right beside him, Joshua curled up with his hands covering his face to keep the bugs away. Then he zoomed out in his mind, his brother shrinking into the blackness of the forest, getting smaller and smaller. But that made him feel lonely. So he closed his eyes and listened for the distant hum that meant there were people not all that far away.

But there was only silence.

"It's stopped," said Virgil.

"What?" asked Kaitlyn.

"The noise."

She listened too, eyes staring as she turned her head.

To Virgil it was an awful disappointment. As usual, he imagined the worst thing first, that the people had gone away and there was no hope that Joshua would ever find them. But Kaitlyn said the silence was nothing to worry about.

"It's dark now," she said. "Nobody works in the dark."

"Okay. Maybe," said Virgil.

"You'll see. Josh will get up before dawn and start moving again. He'll find the people—or they'll find him—and someone will come along first thing in the morning. Probably just after daylight."

Something in her voice made Virgil think she was only trying to cheer him up, to keep him feeling hopeful. But a strange thought stirred in the back of his mind. It was like one of those grubs on the stick, a nasty thing wriggling to the surface. He hoped that no one would come along. He wanted to fix the van and drive out to the highway. He wanted to be the hero.

Kaitlyn lit the fire. Gas came hissing from the BIC lighter, and the flame crackled up through the wood, shining on her skin with a yellow glow.

She and Virgil finished the can of soup they'd opened that morning, then leaned back and watched the wood burn.

"Do you think we'll ever come back?" asked Kaitlyn.

Virgil didn't understand. "Back to where?"

"To Little Lost Lake. Do you think we'll ever take Mom's ashes there?"

"I don't know," said Virgil. He hadn't thought about that. "Maybe not in Rusty, but—"

"I don't think so." Kaitlyn pulled a bigger branch from the pile of wood. "Dad will never let us come back alone. And he's never going to want to go with us."

"So what about Mom's ashes?"

"They'll just sit around," said Kaitlyn. "Dad will keep

them on a shelf for a while. Then he'll move them to a closet, and pretty soon he'll forget all about them."

"No," said Virgil. "He can't keep Mom in a closet."

"They're just ashes, Virg."

He had told himself the same thing. His mind knew it was true, but his heart felt differently. "They're *Mom*'s ashes," he said. "She wanted them scattered on the lake, so that's what we have to do."

"Well, I'm not sure it's all that important. I think—"

Kaitlyn never got to say what she was thinking. From the forest came that same scream they'd heard the night before.

18

Don't wait; Just go.

The scream was louder and closer than ever. It came as such a shock to Virgil that the little stick he was holding flew from his hand and spun away into the dark.

A moment later it came again, a shrieking that tingled inside him.

"I can't listen to this anymore," said Kaitlyn. She chose the biggest branch in Virgil's pile of firewood and levered herself to her feet.

"Don't go out there!" cried Virgil.

"Don't worry!" she said. "I'm not going to."

She tucked one end of the branch under her arm and turned a slow, hobbling circle. Virgil stood beside her, and they heard the thing that was out there moving through the forest. It went as quietly as a whisper, with a slithering sigh as it brushed against leaves.

"It's coming closer," said Virgil.

"Build up the fire!" said Kaitlyn. "It might scare it away."

In handful after handful, Virgil piled all the wood he had found onto the flames. He tossed in the green branches and the moldy sticks, hoping to fill the darkness with a glare of light. But he only made smoke. It rose in thick, churning clouds that hid the forest and the van and nearly everything else. He could barely see his sister, only two feet away.

But he could hear that thing creeping toward them. It slid between the trees, rasping on the bark.

"Get in the van," said Kaitlyn. She gave Virgil a push. "Run!"

But he wouldn't go without her. He tried to take her arm and pull her along.

"Don't wait," she cried. "Just go!"

It would have been so easy to do that. In less than five seconds he could reach the van and lock himself inside. But he couldn't leave Kaitlyn alone in the smoky darkness. He put his arm around her waist and tried to hold her up.

She lurched toward the van in tiny steps, inches at a time. With both hands, she swung the branch forward, then hopped up beside it and swung it again. Step by step, with a scrape and shuffle, she moved so slowly that Virgil wanted to yell at her to hurry. But he knew she was going as fast as she could.

The thing screamed again. The sound was so loud that the creature might have been right behind them—or right beside them; there was no way to tell in the dark and the smoke. It raced through Virgil's body like an electric shock. And it made Kaitlyn move faster.

She dropped her branch and clutched onto Virgil, and they stumbled along together. When they reached the van they reeled to the doorway and tumbled inside. Virgil slammed the door and locked it. He moved from window to window, peering out at the smoke-filled night.

"Do you think it'll try to get in?" he asked.

"No, we're safe here," said Kaitlyn.

They sat in the dark and waited for that thing to leap up at a window. They listened for it crunching across the gravel, for its claws to screech across the metal. And the waiting was the worst thing of all.

"Play a song on your phone," said Virgil.

"I can't," she told him.

"Why not?"

"I gave it to Josh. I thought he might need it for backup if his battery runs out."

"You want to listen to the radio?"

"It won't work out here," said Kaitlyn. "We're too far from the city."

"There's always stuff at night."

She didn't turn away from the window. "Try it if you want."

Virgil squeezed into the front seat and fumbled along the dashboard to find the ignition key. The radio dial lit up in orange and red, and when he turned the knob the speakers hummed and crackled. With a twist of the tuner, he found a man quoting from the Bible. With another, he was picking up a fellow yelling about a hockey game. One after the other, garbled voices squawked in the darkness, fading in and out like spirits in a séance. Then Elvis Presley was singing "Don't Be Cruel" in a voice that was clear and loud.

"Let's listen to that," said Kaitlyn.

The signal came from a thousand miles away, skipping across the stratosphere and down again. A man who called himself "the Snake" played music that was old before Virgil was born. The names sounded funny. Chubby Checker. The Fleas. Tippie and the Clovers.

Virgil didn't like the music. It was full of blaring trumpets and saxophones. But Kaitlyn lay on the back seat and danced with her hands until even that movement made her ankle ache.

Virgil switched on the lights. They turned the windows into mirrors and made the canvas glow. They made him feel safe again.

When the Snake played Buddy Holly, Kaitlyn tried to sing along. Virgil began to sway with the music, and Rusty rocked on squeaky hinges. They forgot all about the thing that was waiting outside.

But it slammed against the van.

Whatever it was, it was big enough to make a sledgehammer sound on the metal. It made the van lurch so violently that Virgil fell off the driver's seat.

He hauled himself up and tried to look out through the windshield. A pale, terrified face was staring back at him, but it was only himself reflected in the glass. Then Kaitlyn switched off the lights and the face vanished, and in the glimmer of the radio dial Virgil looked out at a black world lit only by the orange eye of the dying fire. There was no starlight, no moonlight, no difference between forest and sky.

"Turn on the headlights," said Kaitlyn.

Virgil pulled the switch and gasped at what he saw.

Smoke swirled over the road. The headlights pierced through it in flaring, yellow beams. Twenty feet away, a huge bear was lumbering across the road.

From the radio came a beating of drums and the brassy blare of a horn. The bear swung its head lazily to look right in at Virgil as it plodded past in front of him. Its enormous paws flattened on the road. Its black hair rippled. Swaying from side to side, it stepped out of the beam of light and vanished into the smoke.

"Wow," said Kaitlyn.

Virgil pointed. "Look at that."

Farther along the road, a deer was bounding through the beams of light, up into one and down through the next. In two jumps it crossed the road and disappeared. Other animals followed in straggling bunches, just as the birds had passed. There were raccoons that shuffled along, squirrels that darted, and a tiny mouse that scurried with its nose down. An elk. A deer on stilt-like legs. A hopping frog and a snake that slithered—they came up from the forest and over the road, into the valley of the Bigfoot River.

"What's going on?" asked Virgil.

"I don't know," said Kaitlyn.

"It's like they're heading for Little Lost Lake."

It seemed almost magical to Virgil. First the glorious sunset, then the birds passing by, and now the creatures of the forest trekking up the valley. He believed that all of nature was paying tribute to his mom. But he knew she wouldn't have believed that herself. She would have called the idea "moonshine on the water."

"Hey, Virg, what's that?" asked Kaitlyn.

Virgil peered through the windshield. "What?"

"That shadow."

As far down the road as the headlights could reach, there was a smudge in the smoke. Something was standing in the middle of the road.

"It looks like a person," said Kaitlyn.

Virgil pulled the little lever on the steering column to switch the headlights up to high beams. But instead of piercing farther down the road, they glared back from the smoke and blinded him. So he flicked the switch again.

The figure was gone.

The only thing out on the road was a skunk. With its tail held stiffly upright, it hurried through the light and into the darkness. The music from the radio faded out. It roared back for a moment and faded again before "Great Balls of Fire" blasted from the speakers. Out on the road, animals kept straggling by. Virgil watched them for a long time, until Kaitlyn said, "I think the lights are going out."

She was right. They had faded so slowly that Virgil hadn't noticed. But now they were pale and yellow, and they didn't reach half as far as they had before. The battery was dying.

"You'd better shut them off," said Kaitlyn.

And he did.

19

The Witching Hour

It was the witching hour on Headless Mountain. The down-slope winds of a hot summer day were shifting in the cooler air. Unsettled, they whirled across the mountain-side in whistling gusts.

The fire crews had been flown out for the night, leaving the Beast prowling below the stone walls of El Malvado.

The wind tore the flames from burning trees and whipped them round and round. It made roaring twists of fire and sparks and stretched them up to enormous heights. Burning branches soared up the cliffs and tumbled down into the forests above them. In a moment, the Avalanche Fire was out of control.

Pulled by the wind to the crowns of the trees, the flames bounded through the forest. They jumped across the fire breaks and stormed over the mountain at seven miles an hour.

The Beast had escaped from its cage.

20

The Burning Valley

Almost two thousand feet up, just below the summit of Headless Mountain, Joshua Pepper stopped for a rest. He sat at the foot of a cliff he couldn't climb in the dark and waited for daylight to let him go on.

In the huge valley of the Bigfoot below him, there was only a single spot of yellow light. He thought it was Rusty's canvas roof lit from inside the van, and he imagined that he was looking right through the cloth at Virgil and Kaitlyn. The thought made him feel a little less lonely in the blackness that surrounded him. But a few minutes later, in another part of the valley, a pair of headlights appeared.

They merged into a single beam that was broken into a dotted line by the trees. He imagined that it was mist from the Bigfoot River that made them hazy and faint, and his first thought was that someone was driving down the Boneyard, that help was on the way for his brother and sister.

But the lights weren't moving. They seemed fixed in place, a silver pin jabbed into the valley floor.

It took Joshua a few minutes to figure it out. The headlights were Rusty's, but the first yellow light he'd seen was the Sasquatch museum. From the top of the mountain they looked a long way apart, but there was no other possibility. He wondered if the headlights were meant to guide him, and then who it was who'd thought of switching them on. Probably Virgil, he decided. It was a good idea, though not much help.

For two hours, Joshua watched the beam of light growing shorter and fainter. He could see the mist growing thicker, deeper, spreading through the valley. But still it seemed to him that the lights themselves were fading. When they suddenly disappeared altogether, he felt his old childhood fear of being left alone in the dark. He tried to sleep but couldn't. There were too many flies buzzing around his head, and too many thoughts inside him. He saw the moon rise over the far side of the valley, looking at first like a broken plate split by the jagged horizon. Then it sailed up into the sky, blotting out the stars with its silver glow. Joshua remembered their first night ever at Little Lost Lake, all of them lying in a row on the shore, his mother pointing out the pattern of craters and dusty seas that made up the sorrowful face of the man in the moon. He remembered Virgil asking, "Why does he look so sad?" And their father's reply: "Because he has no one to talk to."

The moon that Joshua watched from Headless Mountain seemed even bigger and brighter. It cast shadows on the ground, and it shone on the mist that lay deep in the valley. Before long, Joshua could see so clearly that he decided not to wait until morning. In the moon's silvery light, he began to climb the cliff.

It wasn't easy. Rocks broke loose when he grabbed them, hurtling past his head to vanish into the dark. He had to test every handhold, every foothold, not trusting a single stone with his entire weight. He oozed up the cliff, moving one arm, one leg, one finger at a time.

When he reached the top and levered himself over the edge, Joshua didn't have the strength to stand up. He lay flat on his stomach till he caught his breath, then slowly rolled over to look down the far side of Headless Mountain.

He hoped to see a logging camp or any other sign of people. The barking of a dog would have pleased him. But what he saw instead only filled him with fear.

The valley was burning.

A line of flames stretched up and down the slopes and gullies. It formed a ragged circle more than a mile across, full of red and yellow smoke. Bursts of fire and sparks exploded inside it, as though bombs were falling on a burning city.

On the top of the mountain, with the fire in front of him, and Virgil and Kaitlyn behind him in the valley of the Bigfoot, Joshua didn't know what to do.

21

A Strange Moon

Virgil lay on the big double bed that had always been his parents' place. His thoughts whirled in a circle, from the thing outside to the broken fitting under the van to his brother way up on the mountain. It seemed impossible, but all their problems had come from a tiny crack in a piece of plastic. There had to be a way to fix it.

His father would get out the duct tape. He might use half a roll, winding it round the fitting in every direction. But that wouldn't work once pressure built up in the cooling system. Uncle Birdy would replace the fitting. He would take something completely nutty, like a part of an old barbecue, and connect the hoses in a way that no one else would have ever imagined. He would get the engine running again, though maybe for only a week. Maybe for only a day. It didn't really matter.

But he couldn't think like Uncle Birdy. Nobody could.

His mom was maybe the only person who would actually repair the fitting. She would take something from here and something from there and make the thing as good as new.

But how?

Virgil tried to imagine everything in the van and how he might use it. The canvas, the curtains, the rubber seals around the doors. The bandages in the first-aid kit. His running shoes and laces. The radio antenna. He invented solutions that even Uncle Birdy wouldn't have dreamed up. But he couldn't imagine any of them actually working, and he was still thinking about it when a pale light appeared in the window. The canvas roof glowed with an orange warmth.

Dawn was breaking. Or so he thought. He had never been happier to see the sun come up. But the light didn't get any brighter, and when Virgil finally sat up to look through the window, he saw a blood red moon hovering over the Boneyard.

Dawn was still hours away.

22

A Light in the Darkness

Up on the mountaintop, Joshua looked down into the burning valley. There were no loggers, no motorcyclists. The only people who might help him were firefighters, and he was not at all sure he could find them before he got caught in the fire himself.

He turned around to go back. But when he looked down the cliff he'd just climbed, he was scared to step over the edge. He remembered how the rocks had crumbled when he touched them, how the tangles of fallen trees had blocked his way in the forest. He remembered the creature stalking him through the forest and wondered if Virgil was right. Could there be such a thing as a Sasquatch?

The whole valley of the Bigfoot seemed empty. There was no light from the museum or anywhere else, no gleam of the river or hint of the Boneyard. The smudge that he'd thought was made of mist was made of smoke instead. It was seeping around the sides of the mountain, flowing from valley to valley, and Joshua was afraid that the fire would follow it. Without the beam of the headlights to guide him, how would he find his way to the van? By the time he got there, Virgil and Kaitlyn might be gone. They would smell the smoke or see the flames and head for safety somewhere. Maybe to Little Lost Lake. Maybe—he thought with a twinge of dread—to the Sasquatch museum.

But what if they didn't? Joshua had told them to stay with the van, and he imagined that Virgil might cling to that rule no matter what. It would be just like Virgil to refuse to leave, to sit there honking the horn in the daylight, flashing the headlights at night, until the flames were right around him. But not Kaitlyn. No matter how much pain she was in, she would lead Virgil to a safe place as soon as the fire came over the mountain. She would tell him, "We have to go right now," and Virgil always did what he was told.

With a sigh, Joshua turned around once more, toward the burning valley. He took his first step down the mountain. But again he stopped. There was something glimmering in the darkness below him. It flashed once. It flashed once more.

Under treetops painted silver by the moon, the forest was nothing but shadows and darkness. Joshua waited for the light to wink again, then peered into the dark with his eyes squinting as he tried to figure out what he was seeing. His mind told him that any light in the forest had to be a good thing. Where there was light, there were people. He started toward it.

He tried to go slowly, picking his way at first over rocks and grass, then among trees as he came down from the summit. But the slope grew steeper, and steeper still, until he was running in the moonlight. Desperate to slow himself down, he grabbed onto trees, bushes, and stumps. He spun around and hurtled on.

He went down three hundred feet, then down two hundred more, until the ground began to flatten. From there, still high above the valley floor, he saw the pulsing glow of the fire between the trees ahead.

DAY THREE—MORNING

23

What Uncle Birdy Would Do

Virgil was awake before Kaitlyn. He listened for the car that she had promised would arrive with the daylight. But there was only the same drone of machines in the distance, though maybe a little bit louder.

When he got up and opened the sliding door, he was greeted by the smell of smoke and a white haze that he blamed on the fire from the night before. He couldn't see the sun, but the sky glowed red above the Boneyard. Virgil remembered the old rule about weather—*Red sky in the morning, sailors take warning*—and hoped that it was true. He wanted clouds to make the day cooler, and rain to bring the water they needed and drive away the blackflies. There wasn't a part of him that didn't itch from their bites.

At the edge of the clearing, Virgil found the stick that

Kaitlyn had dropped in the dark. He stood it by her bed, where she'd find it when she woke.

Half an hour later she came out of the van with the last can of soup, with a spoon in her mouth and another for Virgil. "We can eat half of this," she said. "Someone will come before noon."

Virgil frowned. "You said someone would come first thing in the morning."

"So it's taking a little longer," she said. "But I'm sure they're coming."

Virgil was careful not to scoop out any more soup than Kaitlyn had taken. When they finished, he sucked from his T-shirt the drops that he'd spilled. But he still felt hungry, as though his stomach was tied in a knot.

Kaitlyn tucked the stick under her arm and moved to the grass at the side of the road. Virgil crawled under the van.

"I don't know why you're doing that," said Kaitlyn, as she watched him wriggle underneath the back bumper. "Josh told you it can't be fixed."

He ignored her. Flat on his back, he had to reach up to scrape the dirt from the broken fitting. He could see the crack easily now. Almost an inch long, it grew wider when he twisted the hoses.

It reminded him of the time when he'd taken his broken bicycle to Uncle Birdy.

– – –

The parts of Virgil's bicycle are spread out on the workbench, the bones of a strange skeleton. Uncle Birdy is sorting through them with fingers that are black with oil and grease.

"Here's your problem," he says. "There's a crack in your frame, Virg."

"Can you fix it?"

"You forget who you're talking to," says Uncle Birdy. "There's only two things in the world I can't fix: a broken promise and..."

"The crack of dawn!" He's heard it so often that the words came out exactly as Birdy would say them: the cracka dawn.

Uncle Birdy laughs. "That's right, Virg. Let's weld 'er up."

He gets out his black helmet with its heavy visor. It always make Virgil think of an armored knight. "Hang onto this, will ya, while I get ready."

He puts it on. It falls way over his ears, almost down to his shoulders. He pries up the visor to watch his uncle pulling on the thick gloves with their burned fingertips.

"There's a trick to welding," says Uncle Birdy. "You don't just fill up the crack. You melt the sides and flow 'em together. You make everything one again."

– – –

When Virgil crawled out from under the van, the smell of smoke seemed stronger. His mouth felt dry and dusty, his tongue a wooden slab. He picked a pebble from the road and popped it into his mouth, a trick he'd learned from his mother. "It fools your mouth into making saliva," she'd said. "You don't feel thirsty."

He walked up to Kaitlyn. "I know how to fix it," he said.

"How?" she asked, looking up from the grass.

"I'm going to weld it."

The hopeful expression that had come over her face vanished again. "Okay, Leonardo."

"No, really," he said. "I know how to do it. I'm—"

"The smoke's getting worse," she told him. "You can really smell it now."

Virgil wasn't interested in talking about the smoke. Disappointed by her reaction to his news, he just turned around and walked away. In the middle of the gravel pit, he knelt by the remains of the little fire from the night before. There were still embers down in the ashes, and he piled them with moss and fanned them into flames. Then he heated a knife from Rusty's kitchen drawer, turning the blade round and round in the fire.

When the knife glowed a deep red, Virgil got up and dashed to the van. He squirmed underneath the engine, reached up and grabbed the hose. After staring into the fire, he found it hard to see anything in the shadows above him. But afraid that the knife would cool if he didn't work quickly, he held onto the fitting and stabbed at the crack.

Foul, black smoke drifted among the hoses. With a sizzling sound, a bead of plastic dripped onto the road. Virgil twisted the blade and pushed harder.

When his eyes adjusted to the dark and he saw what

he had done, Virgil felt his heart sink. The little crack had become a slot as thick a nickel. The knife had plunged right through it, and he'd made things worse than when he'd started.

"Oh no!" he said.

Kaitlyn yelled back, "What's wrong?"

Virgil felt like screaming. But he thought of his uncle Birdy working patiently through every problem, never getting angry when something went wrong. "Don't blame the doohickey," he would say in his slow singsong. "The doohickey's not out to get you."

Kaitlyn shouted again. "Virgil, what's the matter?"

"This isn't working," he said.

"You should have listened to Josh."

That made Virgil even more annoyed. But just as his uncle Birdy would have done, he put the knife down in the dirt and thought about the problem. There was only one thing to do: he had to take off the fitting.

From here and there he collected a handful of tools that weren't really tools at all: the dinner knife to loosen the clamps, a fork to pry at the hoses, a chopstick that he thought might be useful for something. For two hours he worked under the van, blackening his hands and scraping his knuckles, sometimes kicking the dirt in frustration. But he got most of the hoses off, and there was only one to go when Kaitlyn called his name.

"What do you want?" he snapped.

"Come and look at this," she said.

"At what?"

"Just come and look, Virgil. Please."

Whatever it was, it made Kaitlyn's voice sound shaky and frightened. The only thing that Virgil could imagine scaring his sister that much was a Sasquatch. But when he scurried out onto the Boneyard and stood beside her, he saw something that scared him even more than Sasquatches.

Across the tops of the trees, he stared at the flat summit of Headless Mountain. It looked like a volcano erupting.

24

The Bucket

A line of flames crawled along the ragged edge of Headless Mountain. Thick smoke streaked across the sky, stretched into streamers by winds a mile high. Virgil thought of his brother walking over the mountain and into a burning forest, and he blamed himself for not seeing the signs of fire: the heat, the lightning, the colors in the sky. His mom would have known what they meant; he was sure of that.

Kaitlyn was standing up, leaning on the branch that she used for a crutch. "Are you sure you can fix the van?" she asked. "'Cause if you can't, we should leave right now."

"Where would we go?" asked Virgil.

"I don't know," she said with a shrug. "Down to Little Lost Lake, I guess."

"That's twenty-six miles."

"Not if we cut through the forest."

"It's still a long way," said Virgil. "You can't walk that far."

"I can if I have to. If you help me."

Virgil tried to imagine the two of them staggering twenty miles through the forest. He glanced toward the fire and wondered if they could even keep ahead of it. No matter what they did, it was coming toward them quickly. At first, fixing Rusty was just something he wanted to do. Now it was something he had to do.

"I'll get the van going," he promised. "I know I can do it."

"But how long will it take?"

"An hour," said Virgil.

He went back to work under the van, twisting the hoses, prying with his makeshift tools. The deerflies crawled on his arms and his ankles, and the day grew hotter than ever.

His hour went by, plus a little bit more. When he finally levered the last hose off the plastic and twisted the fitting free, the smoke was thickening all around. He came out from under the van to find Kaitlyn asleep, twitching like a dog in a dream. Her arms and legs, as brown as chestnuts, were scored with white lines where her fingernails had scratched at the bug bites. Her ankle looked so big and purple that Virgil didn't believe she could walk more than a mile or two.

He didn't wake her. He went into the van and rummaged through the glove compartment, pulling out maps and gas receipts, every bit of paper he could find. He fed it all into the fire and heated his knife till the blade was glowing red. Then he pressed the tip against the fitting, trying to weld the crack.

It might have been that he was in too much of a hurry. Maybe his hand was shaking. Maybe the knife was too hot. Whatever the reason, Virgil ended up with a hole so big that he could stick his finger inside it. He'd made things worse instead of better.

Again he felt like shouting. He could have flung himself down and thrown a little tantrum as though he was four years old. But he just squeezed his eyes shut, balled his hands into fists, and waited until the feeling passed. Then, with a sigh, he went back to the van to look for something to plug the hole.

The noise that he made searching through cupboards woke Kaitlyn. She appeared in the doorway, balanced on one foot, and asked, "Is it fixed?"

"Not yet," said Virgil.

Kaitlyn looked up at him, sad and worried. "Then we'd better start walking."

"I can fix it," he said.

"But what if you don't?" asked Kaitlyn. "That's got to be a big fire, Virg. All those animals we saw, all the birds, they must have been running away from it. We can't be trapped here. We have to head down to Little Lost Lake."

"What if Josh comes back and we're not here?"

"We'll leave a note."

"What if it burns up? Josh wouldn't know where we are. Nobody would."

"Don't you think he'd figure it out?" asked Kaitlyn "Where else are we going to go?"

"Back to the highway. Down to the museum." Virgil pointed in every direction. "Maybe straight for the river."

"We can't get to the river," said Kaitlyn. "It's down in a canyon."

"He might not think of that."

With a big sigh, Kaitlyn looked again toward the mountain. The flames seemed tiny in the distance, a row of fairies dancing on the ridge.

"If you were Josh coming back from the mountain," asked Virgil, "wouldn't you want us to wait for you?"

She thought about that. "Okay," she said. "We'll wait a little longer. But if the van's not fixed real soon, we're going to start walking."

Virgil watched his sister turn around and limp away. She had trouble crossing the tiny gravel pit; how could she ever hike through the forest? But the fire was coming closer, and time was running out. He found the roll of duct tape sealed in his father's sad little tool kit and slipped it over his wrist like a bracelet. Then, without thinking, he reached around the front seat and put his hand on the wooden box with his mother's ashes.

He held it up, wishing she was with him, that she could suddenly appear in the van and tell him what to do. Even out at Little Lost Lake, in the middle of nowhere, she had always found a way to fix anything that broke.

He remembered her fixing the bucket.

- - -

"What happened to the bucket?" asks Mom.

She's holding it up by its wire handle, a bright, red bell swinging from her fingers.

"What's wrong with it?" asks Kaitlyn. She's a little girl in pigtails, with freckles on her nose.

Mom tilts the bucket to let them see the bottom. There's a huge, jagged hole in the plastic. "Who did this?"

With a look of guilt, Dad holds up his hand. "I was trying to put up a clothesline," he says.

"So you stood on the bucket?" cries Kaitlyn.

That makes Mom laugh. "Well, now we'll have to make a new one," she says. "Come and help me, Virgil."

She takes the camping knife and heads down the trail through the forest. He tags along behind her, so small that his eyes are level with his mother's waist. The Oregon grape is a towering wall beside the trail.

They go down to the end of the lake. An aspen felled by the beavers lies half on the ground and half in the water. Mom straddles the trunk and peels off strips of white bark. Virgil rolls them into little tubes, thinking he's a great help.

"Now all we need is some glue," says Mom.

"But there's no store!" shouts Virgil.

"Use your imagination," she tells him, with a pat on the head. "We're in the biggest store in the world. Everything we need is right around us."

– – –

Virgil put the box back on the seat. He walked out to the trees at the edge of the forest and searched for dribbles of sap on the bark. It looked like candle wax hardened into globs and tiny icicles.

At Little Lost Lake, Mom had done the same thing. She had pried off the sap with her camping knife and rolled it into a sticky, sweet-smelling ball. "People used to mix this with moss and use it to patch canoes and all sorts of things," she'd told him. "It sticks like crazy, and it's absolutely waterproof."

With a big glob of sap and a handful of moss, Virgil went back to the van. Above the trees, white smoke was rising in thick plumes where there'd been no smoke before.

"Look at that," said Kaitlyn. "The fire's spreading round the mountain. It's going to cut us off if we don't get out of here soon."

"I've got everything I need," said Virgil.

She stared at the things in his hands, but didn't say a word. She didn't have to. Virgil looked down at the lump of sap and the shreds of moss, at the roll of duct tape around his wrist, and doubted that he'd ever fix the van.

25

Seeing the Light

At the dizzying edge of El Malvado, Joshua trudged south across the side of Headless Mountain. Whorls of smoke twisted around him, gusting up the slope.

He could no longer see the summit or the valley floor below him. But he could hear the fire roaring in the smoke. It had scaled the cliffs and rounded the mountain, heading for the Bigfoot River.

Somewhere ahead, the light still glinted among the trees. But the flashes that had once come steadily were now long minutes apart.

Joshua was sure that someone was signaling to him. He hoped it was a message leading him to safety, the blinking light telling him, "Come here. Come here." But he was growing afraid that it might be a cry for help from someone just as lost as he was himself.

With his arms out in front of him, he staggered along

like a zombie, pushing his way through the bushes. The smoke made him cough, and he stopped now and then just to breathe. But only for a moment. Then he forced himself to walk again, until he came out of the forest at the edge of a chasm, a deep cut in the cliffs.

It was wide and steep, and the bottom—far below him—was covered with boulders and stones. Avalanches had swept away the forest, leaving shattered bits of ancient trees poking through the rubble.

Joshua was looking up and down the gully, wondering how to cross it, when the light flashed from the other side.

He didn't see where it had come from. He waited—and he waited a long time—until he saw it again, a blink of light among the trees. For the first time, Joshua saw exactly where the light was coming from. Across the gully, a few hundred feet below him, a wooden structure stood among the trees.

A fire lookout.

26

The Cardboard Robot

Sitting cross-legged on the gravel, Virgil wrapped strips of duct tape around the fitting. One after the other he layered them on, covering his plug of moss and sap. When he finished, he didn't even want to show Kaitlyn what he'd done. It looked too much like one of his father's repair jobs, an embarrassing wad of gray tape.

In that moment he wished he had listened to Kaitlyn and headed for Little Lost Lake. They might not have gone more than three or four miles, but they would be that much farther from the fire. He should have known better than to try to fix the van. He had imagined something tidy and perfect, but he had ended up with one of his old childish failures.

Virgil remembered the robot. He hadn't thought of it in ages, as though he'd blocked it from his mind. But, suddenly, in his mind, he was nine years old again.

– – –

He's walking home from school with Liam, his best friend. A few yards in front of them, two teenage boys are talking loudly about girls. All along the street, garbage cans stand at the curb, waiting to be picked up in the morning. Beside them are the blue bins for recycling, overstuffed with tin cans and cardboard. Virgil and Liam look into each one, hoping for treasures.

Half a block from his house, Virgil sees what his dad has carried out for recycling. Poking up from the blue box is the robot he made a week ago. Its body is a Cheerios box, its head a juice can with holes hammered out for the eyes. Its arms and legs are the stubby cardboard tubes from rolls of toilet paper.

It's standing up in the box with its arms sticking straight out, and to Virgil it looks sad and lonely, as though it's a child waiting for someone to play with. But when the older boys see it, they laugh. One of them yanks the robot out of the box by one arm and stands it on the sidewalk. It has juice-pack shoes that make it rock back and forth.

"Who made this piece of junk?" asks the kid.

Liam must know. He's been to Virgil's house many times, and they meet outside it every morning. But he doesn't say anything, and Virgil is squirming with embarrassment.

The older boy gives the robot a punch that sends the head clattering across the pavement. The cardboard body rocks backward and topples onto the sidewalk. He kicks the arms off, kicks the legs off, and rams his foot through the cereal box.

Virgil feels shocked, as though he's watching a murder. But as the pieces of the robot go flying, Liam starts laughing so hard that he falls on the ground, nearly hysterical as the robot is slaughtered in front of them.

— — —

With one more look toward the sky, Virgil wriggled back under Rusty's engine. He worried that his repair job was no stronger than his cardboard robot. With a sense of dread, he began connecting hoses.

27

At the Lookout

At the edge of the gully, Joshua waved his arms and shouted, "Hello! Hello!"

But nobody answered, not even an echo. His voice was swallowed by the trees and the smoke.

Sore and tired, Joshua climbed down the cliff and started across the slope. The stones slithered away from under his feet and he went sliding down the slope like a skateboarder, with his arms held out for balance, until he could stop himself. But the stones kept tumbling on without him, leaping down the avalanche chutes and into the burning forest. With every step, he was afraid that he would follow them.

Halfway across, Joshua held onto a shattered tree trunk and stopped for a rest. He could see the cupola at the top of the lookout, its windows shining with reflected light: the gray of the smoke and the red of the flames, and the green of the trees all around. Was that all he'd seen from the distance, he wondered—just the flash of sunlight on a windowpane? He thought he could see someone moving around inside, and he shouted again, "Hello!"

The patterns kept changing on the windows, each pane a kaleidoscope. But nobody shouted back, and nobody came outside to look.

Joshua pushed himself away from the tree and angled across the chute. For every yard he gained, he slid six inches down. Twice he fell on his back and went tobogganing down the mountain, carried along by the stones with his arms flailing. Both times he grabbed hold of a stranded tree, a tiny island on the slope, and held on while the stones kept sliding past. And both times he shouted for help but got no answer from the lookout. When he reached the rocks at the edge of the chute and started climbing, he had an awful fear that no one was there at all.

Covered with dust and scratched by the stones, Joshua tramped up through the forest toward the lookout. It had the feeling of a house long empty, the trail overgrown by bushes, bits of metal left rusting on the ground. At the base of the tower, at the foot of a ladder, Joshua found an old sleeping bag and an empty whiskey bottle with a spider living inside it.

He bent back his head and looked up at the cupola, a hundred feet above him. Always afraid of heights, he told himself that it would be a waste of time to climb the ladder. He'd been following reflections, his signals only the flash of sky and firelight. But he asked himself, what if he was wrong? What if he'd come through the forest and over the mountain only to turn away a hundred feet from help?

There might be a radio.

Just as Virgil would have done, Joshua formed a picture in his mind. He saw the radio—a big old thing in a green metal case—sitting on a shelf in the cupola, a microphone hung on a silver hook with its cord in a tidy coil. He saw a battery under the shelf, a red wire and a black wire waiting to be connected—everything ready just in case somebody needed help.

But the ladder terrified him. The wooden rungs looked old and rotten, and the tower swayed as soon as he started climbing. Halfway to the top, he had to force himself to keep going, to let go of the rung and reach for the next one. Afraid to look up and afraid to look down, he kept his eyes fixed on the ladder. Seventy feet up, he thought he couldn't possibly climb any higher. Eighty feet up, he started wondering how he'd ever get down. But rung by rung he kept going, lifting one hand and then the other, one foot and then the other, and the fire and the smoke whirled in a dizzying blur in the corners of his eyes.

At the top of the ladder was a little trapdoor, a panel set into the floor of the cupola. With his knees trembling, Joshua clutched onto the ladder with one hand as he reached up to lift the door. But it was too heavy to be pushed open that way, and he couldn't climb any higher with one hand holding the door. So he pressed the top of his head against it and pushed it up while he climbed. As soon as the door cracked open, a swarm of flies came streaming from the cupola. They buzzed around him, against his hands and face, tangling in his hair. He couldn't move his head to shake them away or let go of the ladder to swat them. He could only keep climbing, pushing the door until it flopped back on its hinges with a crash and a puff of dust. Another horde of flies shot out through the open hatch.

As Joshua climbed up into the cupola he wondered why it was full of flies. It was only a curious thought, but as soon as he asked himself the question he imagined a terrible answer.

A dead man was sitting inside.

Joshua was sure that he was right. He would find a corpse sitting in a chair, with maggots spilling from his eyes. It was almost enough to make him close the door and climb down as fast as he could. But the thought of the radio kept him going. He pulled himself up to the floor of the cupola and looked around the little room.

There was no dead man staring blindly across the valley. There wasn't even a chair. There was no desk, no shelf, no telephone, and certainly not a radio. There was nothing but the ends of clipped-off wires poking out from a painted wall.

Joshua hauled himself into the cupola and looked down at the burning valley. He couldn't see any way out of it. To the south the fire had climbed up the mountain, and it was closing in from above and below. In an hour—maybe two—it would be burning all around him.

Joshua had never felt so afraid as he did right then. But over the sound of the fire, he heard something that gave him hope. There was a faint rumbling of engines, the chugging drone of a helicopter.

It was growing louder, coming closer.

Joshua raced from window to window, peering out in each direction. The sound grew so loud that the panes of glass rattled in their frames. He felt the thumping of the rotors but couldn't see the helicopter until he put his face against a window and looked straight up. And there it was!

The machine hovered right above him with the rotors blurred into a gray disk. It was drifting sideways above the treetops, rocking from side to side. In helmet and goggles, the pilot was leaning out through an open door, peering straight down.

Joshua waved to him. But he remembered the windows reflecting the light and knew the pilot couldn't see through them. He banged his fists on the glass, trying to shatter the pane, and shouted into the thunder of the rotors. But the helicopter kept sliding away, turning slowly as it skidded above the forest. The tips of the trees bent and shivered in the wind that it made.

Desperately, Joshua launched himself through the trap-door and grabbed onto the ladder.

28

A Thing of Beauty

The wind came up as Virgil lay underneath the van. It made a whispering sound in the tops of the trees and a strange sort of ghostly moan. Flat on his back, with the engine right above him, Virgil was trying to connect the last hose. But it was the hardest of all, barely long enough to reach the fitting. It kept springing out of his hand, whipping back to strike him on the stomach.

He nearly had it in place when Kaitlyn startled him by hammering on the van. The hose flew away and slapped him again.

"We have to go right now," said Kaitlyn.

"Okay!" he said. "I'm almost—"

"No, it's not okay," she told him. "It looks like the sky's on fire, Virgil. We'll die if we stay here."

Virgil thought he was too close to being finished to give

up just then. "Quittin's for kittens," he muttered. Then he grabbed the hose and tried once more.

"Well, *I'm* leaving," said Kaitlyn. "Do you hear me, Virg? I'm heading for the lake, if you want to try to catch up."

Virgil could see only her feet and the tip of her crutch as she hobbled away. In a moment she had vanished around the front of the van. He didn't yell at her to stop, or tell her again to wait, because he was sure she couldn't go very far. He grabbed the hose and jammed it once more at the fitting. He pushed and turned it, and with a little plop it snapped into place.

Virgil could hardly believe he'd done it. He tugged on the hose to make sure, gently at first and then harder. When it didn't spring loose, he smiled to himself.

"Hey, Kait," he shouted, "it's fixed!

There was no answer. But that didn't surprise him. With the sound of the fire rising every moment, she wouldn't have to go far before she couldn't hear him.

Virgil tightened the clamps around the ends of the hoses, using the dinner knife as a screwdriver. Then he rolled onto his stomach and squirmed out to the road, pushing with his elbows in an alligator fashion.

When he stood up on the Boneyard, he was amazed by the smoke. It was a wild river flowing through the sky, churning through the treetops. Burning debris tossed up by the fire made a huge whirlpool of embers and sparks. Virgil couldn't see the flames, but he knew they were close. He could hear them crackling, louder than fireworks. He could see their glow in the smoke, and it was just as Kaitlyn had said. The sky was on fire.

"Kaitlyn!" he shouted. "Kaitlyn, where are you?"

He turned right around, looking along each side of the road, hoping she had sat down to wait for him. Again he called her name, and when she didn't answer he turned once more and dashed across the gravel pit, heading for Little Lost Lake.

He wasn't sure how much time had passed since she'd told him she was leaving. With a broken ankle and a stick for a crutch, she couldn't go very fast. But he was afraid he wouldn't find her with the smoke growing thicker.

Virgil scrambled up the slope. And right at the top, he found Kaitlyn.

She was sitting there with her back against a tree, her ankle looking twisted and torn. She was staring at the smoke as it flowed above the trees.

"Kait, it's finished," he said.

Slowly, she turned her head to look at him.

"I fixed it," he told her. "We can drive away."

There was no emotion in her voice. "That's great, Virg."

He was disappointed by her answer, and he didn't understand why she wasn't excited.

"Look." She pointed toward the fire. "It's almost at the road. We're not going to get away."

"I think we will," said Virgil.

She shook her head. "It's cut us off. That's why no one's come to get us. The whole Boneyard's on fire."

"We've still got time," said Virgil. "Come sit in the van, Kait. I'll fill the water, and then we can go." He reached down to pull her up. "Come on."

She didn't move for just long enough that he thought she *wouldn't* move. Then she picked up the crutch that lay beside her and took his hand. Virgil helped her up, then guided her down the slope and across the gravel pit. But she refused to get into the van. "I'll help you get ready," she said.

"I can do it," he told her.

"We can do it faster together."

At the very back of the van was a small expansion tank. Kaitlyn took off the cap while Virgil brought the water. Careful not to spill a drop, he swung the bucket between his legs while he walked like an old, bowlegged cowboy.

A burning branch fell on the road in front of him. It landed with a *whump* and a hiss of embers. Twists of smoke curled from the tip of each little twig.

Virgil stepped over it. Kaitlyn helped him lift the bucket, and together they poured the water into the tank, nearly gagging from the smell. Wads of tangled hair and tiny chunks of food spilled over the rim and gurgled down through the pipes, into Rusty's rubber arteries.

"That's not very much," said Kaitlyn.

"There's no more. It'll have to do." Virgil dropped the empty bucket on the road and picked up the cap to close the tank. But Kaitlyn stopped him. "Let's use the good water," she said.

"Oh, I don't know," said Virgil. The idea scared him. He didn't know for sure that the van would start. Joshua had said that it would, but Joshua had said as well that it might blow up if they drove it. Kaitlyn was taking a huge chance, gambling their drinking water on his repair job.

"It's okay," she told him. "I trust you, Virg."

She couldn't have said anything that would please him more than that. With a grin on his face, he went into the van and got the Coke bottle. They each took a tiny sip of water. Then Virgil tipped up the bottle and emptied it into the van. But when he peered into the tank, it was empty. Every drop of water had vanished down the pipes.

"It's not leaking out, is it?" asked Kaitlyn.

Virgil wished he'd thought of that before he emptied the bottle. Almost fearfully, he got down on his knees and looked under the van. "No, it's okay," he said. His repair job was working.

"Let's see if it starts," said Kaitlyn.

29

In the Driver's Seat

All along, Virgil had imagined himself driving the van. But he had never told his sister that, and she went straight to the driver's door, hopping on her crutch. She pulled it open, then turned to look back at him.

"Let's go," she said.

Virgil sighed to himself. It didn't seem fair that he had to help her into the driver's seat after he was the one who'd fixed the van. But he knew it had to be that way. Kaitlyn had a learner's permit, and she had practiced with their father. The only time Virgil had sat behind Rusty's steering wheel, he was balanced on his father's lap. And even then he had steered right into a huckleberry bush. He had never worked the gearshift, never pressed the pedals. He told himself it was only right that Kaitlyn did the driving.

"Virg, come on!" she told him. He started for the other

side, toward the passenger's seat. But she shouted at him again. "Where are you going? You have to drive."

That took him by surprise. "Why?" he asked.

"I can't do it with a broken ankle."

Kaitlyn held the door while Virgil climbed up to the seat and wriggled in behind the steering wheel. Though he was twice as old as the last time he'd driven Rusty, his feet still didn't reach the pedals. They dangled below him, making him feel as small as a child in a high chair. Through the windshield, he could see smoke swirling above the trees, colored red by the flames of the fire.

"Take my stick," said Kaitlyn, pushing it into his hands. "You can use it on the clutch."

He didn't want to ask where the clutch was. He took the stick and planted its tip on one of the three pedals.

"That's the brake," said Kaitlyn. She moved the stick to the left-side pedal. "There, that's the clutch. When you hold it down, it keeps the engine out of gear. That's the gas pedal on the other side, the brake in the middle. Now give me the box."

"What box?"

She pointed at the seat beside Virgil. "Mom's ashes."

"What are you going to do with it?"

"Just give me the box!"

Another burning branch, bigger than the first one, fell out of the smoke and burst onto the middle of the gravel pit. It sprang up for a moment and settled again in a smoking heap of embers.

Virgil passed the box to Kaitlyn.

She wedged it against the steering column to hold the gas pedal down. Virgil hated to see it used like that. But he reminded himself that it was only a box, and that the whole reason for being there was to get it down to Little Lost Lake.

On her one good foot, Kaitlyn stepped back and slammed the driver's door shut. She hopped around the front of the van and got in beside Virgil.

"Push down on the clutch," she told him.

Virgil leaned on the stick and pressed the pedal right to the floor. With a crunch of gravel, Rusty rocked forward. Kaitlyn leaned over to work the gearshift, jamming it back and forth. "Okay, I think you're in second," she said. "Now listen, Virg. When the engine starts, it's going to be racing. When I say 'Now,' let the clutch out. But *don't drop the stick* because you'll need it for the brake pedal. It's going to slam into gear, so be ready."

"What about the roof?" asked Virgil. "It's still open."

She glanced up at the big canvas roof. "Let's not worry about it. Just turn the key."

It was still in the ignition. Virgil waited for a moment, going over in his mind what he had to do. He pushed down hard on the clutch pedal and turned the key.

The engine made a grinding sort of groan and turned over once. After that, there was nothing.

"Try it again," said Kaitlyn.

Virgil turned the key off, then on again. A loud click came from the starter. But the engine wouldn't turn over.

"The battery's dead," said Kaitlyn.

30

The Helicopter

From the ladder on the lookout, Joshua watched the helicopter drift above the trees. The tips of the blades were painted yellow, and they drew a circle in the sky. The *whumpa-whumpa* sound of their thrumming beat inside his ears.

He waved one hand as he clung to the ladder, and his clothes flapped in the helicopter's wind. He kept yelling, though no one could hear him.

The helicopter turned away and slid across the tree-tops. Then its nose suddenly lifted, and it swung toward him again. Virgil saw the pilot through the windshield, and beside him was a woman with red hair and a black helmet. She made a hand signal that Joshua didn't understand, then pointed at the ground.

Joshua was afraid he'd get blown right off the ladder if he let go with even one hand. The wind tore needles off the fir trees and whipped them against his cheeks. He pressed his face against the ladder and waited till it eased off.

When he looked again, the helicopter was well below him, swinging across the mountainside with a red light flashing on the tail. A hundred yards away, it started hovering above the forest, then slowly dropped between the trees.

Joshua scrambled down the ladder. He found the helicopter sitting on a platform made of logs. The rotors were whumping round and round, the engine whining softly. The woman opened her door and climbed out. She met Joshua at the edge of the platform, shouting questions at him over the engine's roar. Where had he come from? Was he hurt?

But Joshua had only one thought in his mind. He pointed high toward the mountain's ridge, toward the valley on the other side. "My little brother's over there. My sister too," he said. "They're stranded on the Boneyard at Mile 34. You have to help them. Please."

31

Turn the Wheels!

Virgil blamed himself for the dead battery. Joshua had warned him about it, but he hadn't listened. He'd used the headlights, the radio, and every light in the van. What if he'd spent all that time fixing the van and it couldn't even start?

"So now what?" he asked.

"We can push it," said Kaitlyn. "If we get it moving fast enough we can bump-start it." She opened the door and swung around to get out. "You stay there. I'll push."

"What about your ankle?" asked Virgil. "I should push."

"You're not strong enough."

Kaitlyn slid down from the seat and got out. She held onto the van as she opened the sliding door, then planted one knee on Rusty's floor. With half her body in the van, ready to push with her good foot, she braced herself against the frame. "Ready?" she asked.

"I don't know," said Virgil. "What's going to happen?"

"When I say 'Now,' let the clutch go," she said. "You'll feel a big jolt when the engine starts."

She dug her foot into the gravel and grunted as she pushed hard on the van. Virgil felt Rusty rock forward, then settle back again. He shifted his grip on the steering wheel and looked down to make sure that the stick was right in the middle of the clutch pedal. When he raised his head he saw ribbons of sparks stretched out through the smoke above the Boneyard. Burning twigs cartwheeled high above him, as though carried along by the river of smoke.

"Is the key turned on?" asked Kaitlyn.

Virgil glanced down. "Yes."

Kaitlyn rose up on her knee and pushed again. As slow as a snail, Rusty inched forward. Gravel crunched under the tires.

The van moved a little faster, then a little faster again. To Virgil it seemed too big and too heavy, an elephant that he couldn't control. As though by itself, it drifted off toward the side of the road.

"Turn the wheels!" shouted Kaitlyn.

He cranked the steering wheel. Rusty straightened out and rolled along the Boneyard. The needle on the speedometer climbed up toward five. Kaitlyn was pumping her leg, pushing hard with each step.

"Now!" she shouted.

32

Flying Out

The helicopter soared across the mountain's ridge. The nose dropped, and it plunged into the valley. Joshua, in the back seat, felt himself spinning down through the smoke and thought they were crashing. He saw the pilot fighting with the controls, looking like a spider in his big helmet, both arms and both legs moving at once. Only the woman sitting quietly in the left-hand seat prevented him from panicking. Her hands were folded in her lap, her head tilted as she looked calmly through the window.

They had given him orange earmuffs, huge and clunky, to muffle the deafening noise of the helicopter. But he couldn't talk to the pilot or woman, and couldn't hear a word of what they were saying to each other.

As the helicopter leveled off, the sense of free fall ended. Joshua saw shadowed trees below him, and then the gray slash of the Boneyard. The helicopter turned to follow it. Far ahead, flames were leaping high into the air.

The pilot spoke to the woman. She nodded and turned to Joshua. Shouting so he would hear, she said, "We're watching for mile markers."

33

Down the Boneyard

The van rumbled along as Kaitlyn pushed, going faster every moment. Half in the van and half outside it, she swung her foot forward and kicked at the gravel, then swung her foot forward again. Virgil struggled with the steering wheel to keep old Rusty running straight.

"Now!" shouted Kaitlyn. "The clutch!"

Virgil let go of the stick. The clutch pedal sprang up from the floor, and the van slammed into gear. For an instant it jarred to a stop, throwing Virgil against the steering wheel. Then it leaped forward with the engine racing, and he was flung back into the seat again. Rusty veered to the edge of the road, then skidded back the other way as Virgil spun the steering wheel. In a clatter of gravel and a cloud of dust, they slithered down the Boneyard in a dusty whirlwind until Virgil got it under control.

"Woohoo!" he cried. "We did it!"

He glanced back at Kaitlyn, beaming.

But she wasn't there.

He saw a shape in the mirror, a tumbling shadow in the cloud of dust. Then the bend in the road was suddenly right in front of him, and trees were filling the windshield. He hauled on the steering wheel and slid sideways into the turn. Desperate to stop the van, he grabbed Kaitlyn's stick and jabbed at the brake pedal.

Nothing happened. He jabbed again, driving the pedal right down to the floor. But Rusty kept speeding along.

Virgil shouted. He actually yelled at the old van. "Why won't you stop? What's wrong with you now?"

He couldn't understand why the brakes would stop working just because the engine overheated. Unless it had nothing to do with the engine. He remembered Joshua banging around under the van, trying to find a hose for the distiller. Had he cut the brake lines?

Virgil pushed down on the pedal again. But it made no difference. If anything, the van went faster, kicking up gravel and dust as it raced down the Boneyard.

"Oh, please stop!" shouted Virgil. He swung the stick back and forth, trying to knock away the box that was holding the gas pedal down. But it clanged against the clutch and slipped from his hand, falling to the floor.

In the back, the engine howled with a sound he'd never heard before. Rusty skittered over the potholes, and the needle on the speedometer kept climbing round the dial. Forty miles an hour. Fifty miles an hour.

Virgil felt out of control. The van was a shrieking, rattling thing that couldn't be stopped. It slithered through the next turn with one back wheel riding up onto the grass. Then it swerved across to the other side as Virgil tried to straighten out. He couldn't see the stick; he couldn't reach the box. All he could do was keep steering.

Yellow signs went flying past: 39, 40. The road curved to the right and crested a hill, and Virgil looked down at the Trickleback bridge. It seemed even more narrow than he remembered, more dangerous than his mom had ever imagined. His father had always crossed it at ten miles an hour, and Virgil was racing down the hill at sixty.

He aimed for the middle of the bridge as Rusty skittered through the potholes. The canvas thrummed on the open roof, and on the dashboard a warning light glowed bright red.

The van swerved to the left. Virgil straightened out. The bridge was coming at him too quickly. He felt the thump of Rusty's front wheels going from gravel to wood, but the back end kept sliding. The tires screeched across the wood as Virgil struggled with the steering wheel. Then the bridge was behind him, and the road was rising, turning again.

Dust boiled in through the open door as Virgil went blasting down the Boneyard. He steered round another bend and saw the forest burning on both sides of the road.

34

What's Down There?

The helicopter tilted from side to side. When the woman pointed out a yellow sign, the pilot dropped toward it. Right down among the trees, with little dust devils whirling on the Boneyard, he maneuvered back and forth until she read the number.

Joshua couldn't see it. He tapped the woman's shoulder and yelled when she turned around, "Where are we?"

She signaled with her fingers, holding up three and then one to tell him the mileage on the road. The pilot went soaring up again.

Nose down, the helicopter fluttered along above the Boneyard. As the smoke grew thicker the pilot flew lower, until the skids were nearly brushing the tops of the trees.

The woman turned to shout at Joshua. "We're low on fuel. Fifteen more minutes. Then we turn back."

Buffeted by the wind, the helicopter veered in all directions, and the pilot fought to keep it level.

The woman pointed down.

With his left hand, the pilot pulled the lever in front of him. With his right, he hauled on another beside him. His feet pushed on the pedals, and the helicopter reared up, spinning to the left. Joshua felt himself whirled around as though on a midway ride.

They hovered above the road, bobbling up and down. The helicopter rocked sideways, and in that moment Joshua saw the little clearing where he'd stopped the van. He saw the bit of yellow that had caught the woman's eye. But it wasn't a mile marker. It was a bucket—the new bucket—rocking gently on the road in the helicopter's draft.

The woman shook her head and said something to the pilot. She gestured, and the helicopter started rising.

Joshua leaned forward and tapped her shoulder again. "That's our bucket," he said. "This is where we parked."

Their heads were so close together that the woman's hair rubbed his cheek. But she couldn't hear him, or couldn't understand, and the helicopter kept moving.

"Go back!" yelled Joshua.

The woman touched her helmet to show that she couldn't hear. Joshua practically screamed. "That's our bucket! Go back."

She nodded, then turned to the pilot. He spun the machine around and hovered above the clearing. Very slowly, the helicopter revolved like a weather vane.

The woman shook her head at Joshua. She mouthed words so clearly that he heard them in his mind. "Nobody here."

The treetops beside him bent and swayed. Blown by the rotors, the yellow bucket went skittering away, bouncing across the gravel.

Joshua tried to understand. He knew they were in the right place. So what had happened?

The only thing that made sense was that someone had come along and towed the van away. It could have been a logger in a hauling truck or someone in a big RV, not that it mattered. Just the thought itself was a huge relief. When the woman held up ten fingers to show how many minutes were left, he nodded at her. There was nothing to see; it was okay to leave.

She formed each word slowly, pointing at the ground with each one. "We'll search down the road."

The engine accelerated. Its whine became a scream. The pilot pulled the collective and pushed a pedal, and the helicopter swung up through the smoke.

But the woman started swinging her arms, waving him down again. And as the helicopter dipped and turned, Joshua saw Kaitlyn stumbling from the forest. "That's my sister!" he shouted.

Kait crossed the clearing at half a run and half a hop, with her long hair tangled by the downdraft. In the middle she stopped and looked up, waving wildly as she balanced on one foot.

The pilot circled round her. Kaitlyn pivoted along with him, keeping the helicopter right in front of her. It skidded sideways and slowly descended. Around the clearing, the fir trees bent backward like frightened people.

Kaitlyn crouched on the ground, head down in the cloud of dust and grit raised by the rotors.

- - -

The helicopter soared up between the trees with Kaitlyn lying across the back seats. Her legs lay across Joshua's lap, and her broken ankle was propped up on a bundle of rope. She stared through the window at fiery tornadoes whirling a hundred feet into the air. Smoke stretched as far as she could see.

Nose down, the helicopter followed the Boneyard toward Little Lost Lake. Kaitlyn tried to guess how fast they were flying, how far they were going. When the pilot started hovering over one spot, she imagined that they were more than ten miles down the road. She pulled herself up to get a better look.

It was an unforgettable sight, the fire so close that the flames stretched above her. The smoke was a dark, swirling dome high above the Boneyard, the ground a mass of orange and yellow. In the fire's wind, the helicopter rocked and pitched.

In the front, the pilot and the woman were fixated by something she couldn't see. They were talking through their headsets and microphones, gesturing at the ground. Kaitlyn pulled Joshua down toward her and shouted at him, "What are they looking at?"

He told her with a shrug that he didn't know. Then he touched the woman's shoulder to get her attention. "What's down there?" he yelled. "What do you see?"

She had a haunted look on her face, her eyes wide with fear or wonder. But instead of answering, she looked away and talked to the pilot.

"Let me look!" cried Kaitlyn.

35

The Danger Zone

Rusty slid through the bend and drove straight into the fire. On either side, the forest was burning. Whole trees stood wrapped in flames. And just up ahead, one was falling across the road. It leaned at a terrible slant, with fire and embers raining down on the Boneyard.

Virgil saw the tree toppling and tried to swerve out of the way. A front tire hit the gravel bank, and Rusty rocketed across the road.

The tree fell, crashing into another one with an explosion of sparks. Locked together, they swayed back and forth as Virgil sped underneath them. A branch snagged in the canvas roof and tore it open from end to end. The tree rolled sideways and smashed onto the Boneyard right behind Rusty.

Suddenly, there was no going back. Virgil had been trying all along to stop the van, but now his only fear was that it wouldn't keep running. He steered down the middle of the road, through fire and smoke, telling Rusty, "Don't quit now!"

The red light flashed on the dashboard. Virgil glanced at the temperature gauge and saw the needle pushed into the danger zone. It was quivering as though it might snap.

The heat from the fire pressed in through the windows. It scorched the paint off the side of the van. Burning branches somersaulted through the sky and bounced off the open roof. They covered the road so thickly that Virgil couldn't avoid them. They thumped under the wheels and sprang up against the floor, showering sparks from under the van. Virgil thought of the gas tank underneath him, a metal box three quarters full.

He was riding a bomb through the fire.

36

A Shattered Wreck

Kaitlyn was worried. The people in the front seats did nothing to let her look straight down. It was as though they were trying to stop her from her doing that, and she wondered what they were seeing that they didn't want her to see as well.

Ignoring the pain in her ankle, she squirmed on the seat, pulling herself up to the window. The trees all around were burning from trunk to tip. Whole branches broke off and tumbled away into smoke.

The pilot pulled up, turning to the right. The rotors thrashed through the air with a fluttering growl, and—just for a moment—the helicopter tilted so far that Kaitlyn could look straight down at the Boneyard.

Rusty was there. The van was lying on its side, a shattered wreck with bits and pieces spread for yards along the gravel.

The roof had been peeled back like the lid of a can. The canvas was shredded into long strips that flapped in the wind like old prayer flags.

The woman with red hair swung round in her seat. She shouted at Kaitlyn and Joshua, forming each word carefully to yell with her lips, "We're going to try to land."

37

It's Fear That Will Kill You

Into a gulley and up the other side, through bend after bend, Virgil struggled to keep Rusty on the road. He skidded through a turn with the wheels chattering on the gravel, through another with so much dust welling around him that dust was all he could see. When it faded away, the forest was green again, the fire behind him.

A flash of yellow on the roadside was the marker for Mile 43. *Seventeen more miles to go*, thought Virgil. He told himself that he would get to Little Lost Lake if the van kept running. He would sit by the cool water till the fire passed over, and if he had to he would swim out to the middle of the lake and watch the forest burn.

But what about Kaitlyn? What about Josh? Virgil realized with a pang of guilt that he had started thinking only of saving himself.

You can't help them, he thought. *There's no way to go*

back. They were on their own, the two of them, and the only hope was that they would somehow meet at Little Lost Lake. The only thing he could do was keep going.

The needle on the temperature gauge pushed right over the end of the dial. Up through the vents on the dashboard came clouds of white steam. They billowed over the windshield, coating the glass with white condensation. As Virgil took a hand from the wheel, a stink of oil suddenly filled the van, and the engine made terrible rattling sounds.

"No!" shouted Virgil. "Please don't stop."

He rounded a bend and went over a hill, and again the fire was right ahead of him. A line of flames bounded through the treetops like a stampeding herd of fiery animals.

The red light blinked on and off, on and off. The needle was a trembling finger pointed at the highest temperature on the gauge. Two hundred and fifty degrees.

Virgil remembered his father noting with fear that the gauge had gone that high. It was the only time they'd ever seen the needle reach the danger zone, and Virgil slipped back to that day as he remembered his father shouting.

– – –

It's a hot summer day in Montana. Rusty is three miles from the summit of Beartooth Pass, and almost a mile in the sky.

"Uh-oh," says Dad.

"What's wrong?" asks Mom.

"Seems we're overheating."

Behind the plexiglass on the instrument panel, a red light is flashing slowly.

Dad wants to pull over, to "give the engine a rest," he says. But a dozen cars are pressed up behind him, honking like a flock of geese, and there's no place to pull over. So he keeps going, with poor Rusty shuddering up the hill in low gear.

Virgil, in the back, watches the temperature needle quiver and twitch.

"I don't care for this," says Dad. "I don't care for this at all."

The needle reaches the red-colored part of the dial. Dad cries out, "She's going to blow!"

But nothing happens. Rusty crawls all the way to the Beartooth summit and starts down the other side. Dad eases to the edge of the road to let the cars behind him go roaring past. The needle swings back, the red light goes out, and everything's normal again.

Mom has her window rolled down, letting the wind pull at her hair as she gazes at the mountains. "This is beautiful," she says, as though nothing has happened. But Dad's as shaky as the temperature needle, his face covered in sweat that's not from the heat. He talks as though they'd miraculously survived an awful disaster. "Remind me never to come this way again," he says.

"What would have happened if she blew, Dad?" asks Virgil.

His father's sweaty hands squeak on the steering. "You don't want to know, Virgil."

"But—"

"Let's just leave it at that. You don't want to know."

- - -

Virgil was sure he was about to find out what would happen when an engine blew, and it scared him not to know.

He barreled down the Boneyard in a stench of steam and boiling antifreeze, clinging to the steering wheel as tightly as his dad had done on Beartooth Pass. The red light blinked faster and faster, and the engine banged like a jackhammer. Virgil turtled his head down on his shoulders and whipped the van through the turns in the road.

He saw flames ahead, and then flames beside him. At fifty miles an hour he rumbled over a washed-out culvert that nearly bounced him from his seat.

And then the engine blew.

There was a bang as loud as a gunshot, a screech of metal, and a violent shaking that ran right through the van. Rusty skidded sideways across the road and tipped up on two wheels.

To Virgil, it seemed like a long, slow moment, as unreal as a dream. He saw the trees tilting in the windshield, the grassy roadside falling away from his side window. He felt himself floating from the seat, and he held onto the steering wheel so he wouldn't go drifting away.

The next thing he knew, he was dangling from it, swinging forward and back with his feet in the air and a throbbing pain in his hip. The van was lying on its side with the passenger's door pressed against the gravel. Every cupboard had opened and every drawer had fallen out, their contents scattered all over the place. The windshield had shattered into hundreds of tiny squares that lay glistening on the road. The sliding door had scraped up gravel like a bulldozer's blade and shoveled it into the van.

When Virgil let go of the steering wheel, he landed in a heap on the passenger's door, scrunched between the seat and the dashboard. Everything seemed dreamlike and hazy, and it confused him to have his world turned sideways. He crawled around the dashboard and out through the gaping windshield, pushing aside the last bits of glass.

Enormous clouds of smoke were rolling toward him, tumbling over the forest. The sound of the fire was a dragon's roar, so loud that it had to be nearly on top of him. He thought of hiding in the van and letting it burn its way by. But when he looked back and saw Rusty lying in a puddle of oil, with the roof twisted and broken and everything reeking of gasoline, he decided to run instead.

But which way to go?

He could head straight through the forest for Little Lost Lake. But that was almost twenty miles, and he might lose his way. He might wander in circles till the fire caught him. He could walk downhill to the Bigfoot River. It would be hard to miss that. But it flowed through a canyon with perpendicular walls, and he would never get down to the water. Or he could follow the Boneyard to the Sasquatch museum. It would be the closest place, and the easiest to reach, though he wasn't sure how far he'd have to walk to get there. But it was so creepy. He thought of the skulls hanging from the fence.

Virgil had three choices, and he didn't like any of them. But he had to decide which scared him the least: the forest, the cliff, or the Bugaboo Man.

He chose the forest. If he stayed between the river and the road and kept heading west, he would find his way to Little Lost Lake.

With his mind made up, Virgil waded through the grass at the edge of the road and into the forest beyond it.

Every step was painful. His hip hurt so badly that he stopped to look at it, hooking a finger into the top of his pants to push down the waistband. He saw a bruise as big as a baseball, but it didn't look nearly as bad as Kaitlyn's ankle, and she had never complained. So he ignored the pain and kept on walking.

The forest felt strangely abandoned, but not quite empty, haunted by something he could feel but not see. The things he had read about in Kaitlyn's book prickled at his mind: the Sasquatch, the headless men, the thing that had screamed in the dark. He heard her whispered warning: "a maniac with a machete."

If not for the fire behind him, Virgil couldn't have kept going. He would have turned around and gone back to the road and sat by the wreck of the van until somebody came along. If it took a week it wouldn't matter. Though hungry and thirsty, though lonely and scared, he would wait forever if he had to, a little lost dog at the side of the road.

But the fire was coming after him, tearing through the forest faster than he could ever run. So he forced himself to go slowly.

His mother had taught him that. He remembered her doing it.

- - -

He's walking through the woods at Little Lost Lake, his hand wrapped by his mother's fingers.

"Are your eyes still closed?" she says.

"Yes," he tells her.

"Don't open them yet."

They walk for maybe fifteen minutes, Virgil trailing behind his mom, knowing that nothing bad will happen as long as he holds her hand. He hears a squirrel chattering behind him, a woodpecker drumming above him.

"Okay. Open your eyes," says Mom.

She lets go of his hand. He looks around the forest with no idea where they are.

"Which way do we go to get back?" she asks.

"I don't know," he says.

"Use your eyes," she tells him. "Use your ears. Use that brain of yours."

He imagines there's a secret that he doesn't know, something she hasn't taught him yet. It will be something amazing, a code he can crack by watching butterflies or beetles, one of those fabulous things he can learn only from her.

But all he can think of doing is yelling for his sister. He turns back his head and shouts—"Kaitlyn!"—and she answers from not that far away. "What do you want?" Virgil points toward the sound and says, "We go that way."

His mother laughs. "Well, that's not what I had in mind," she says. "But I guess it will do for now."

Virgil leads the way, blunders through the bushes, heading straight toward the sound of his sister's voice.

"You're going to walk in circles if you don't look where you're going," says Mom. "Pick two trees straight ahead and keep them in line. When you get close to the first one, pick another. Always keep two in line."

He does what she tells him, looking not just where he's putting his feet but where he wants to go. In a few minutes he spots Rusty's open roof up ahead.

"Good work," says Mom. "Now what's the most important thing you learned?"

He's not sure, so he guesses. "To keep trees in line?"

"No," says Mom. "It's to keep your wits. People panic when they get lost. They stop thinking and start running, and if you let that happen you'll never get home. It's fear that will kill you."

- - -

Virgil tried to imagine that his mom was right behind him, just where she'd been that day at the lake. He kept lining up trees as he plowed through currant bushes that were up to his waist. He remembered his mother saying, "See, it's not so hard."

Then he groaned and turned around.

He had forgotten to bring the ashes.

DAY THREE—AFTERNOON

38

The Burning Period

The Beast raged through the valley of the Bigfoot River. It reached long fingers into the gullies and up to the ridges, as though—blinded by its own smoke—it was groping for things that might be hiding there.

There hadn't been a fire in the valley for fifty years. The forest was old and withered, overdue for a burning. It was choked with dead trees, both standing and fallen, that made food for the Beast. In the heat of the afternoon, in what firefighters call "the burning period," it consumed an acre of forest every seven minutes.

It had grown strong enough now to make its own wind, and it spun two-ton trees high in the air. The firefighters didn't have a hope of getting anywhere near it.

Loose in the valley, the Beast was on a rampage.

39

The Wooden Box

An avalanche of smoke rolled over the forest. It buried the trees one by one by one, then buried Virgil too.

It choked him. It blinded him. With watering eyes he struggled to keep the trees in line as they faded away in front of him.

When an orange glow appeared ahead, he thought the sun was breaking through the smoke. He surged ahead, hoping to come out into clear air. But it wasn't the sun he was seeing. It was the fire. A wall of flames stretched through the forest in front of him.

Virgil started running. It was going against what his mom had taught, and it made his hip hurt badly. But he had to reach the road before the fire did. He had to get to the van—and get away again—or the wooden box would be lost forever.

"Forget the ashes," a voice whispered in his mind.

"They're not important." For sure, his mother would have told him not to risk his life for a wooden box. She would hate to think he was doing that. But Virgil would not run away and leave the ashes behind. It would feel as though he was leaving his mom to burn in the fire.

The smoke swirled around Virgil as he trudged along. When he stepped out onto the grass at the edge of the Boneyard, he saw the fire glowing in the trees. He imagined it was watching him, waiting for the right time. It was feeding on the trees to give itself strength to attack.

He thought he would grab the box and head right back into the forest. But Rusty wasn't there.

That frightened Virgil almost as much as the fire. If he couldn't find the van after walking a hundred yards, how would he ever find Little Lost Lake? He didn't even know if he should go left or right to find the van. He looked up and down the road, hoping it would appear in the smoke.

"Use your eyes. Use that brain of yours."

There were no tire tracks in the gravel. No one had driven on that bit of road for a very long time. So Virgil turned to his left and walked down the Boneyard, and he found the van around the next bend. It felt warm when he touched it, like a sleeping animal.

Broken glass crunched under his feet as Virgil stepped through the windshield. The wooden box was still jammed firmly against the gas pedal, and he had to pry it loose with Kaitlyn's stick. The wood creaked and crackled, and when the box fell into his arms Virgil felt such awful sadness that he could have sat down and cried. He didn't know if he would ever see his father again, or his brother or his sister, and he missed his wonderful mom so much that he could hardly bear it. Soon Rusty would be gone as well, and that too seemed sad to Virgil. The old van was a lot more than metal and plastic and canvas. It was almost like part of the family.

Virgil squirmed round the seats and into the back of the van. He picked through the rubble spilled from cupboards and drawers, looking for something to wrap around the box.

The fire's hot wind gusted through the van, flapping the ragged shreds of the canvas roof. Virgil heard it raging toward him and looked out to see it. He turned first to the windshield, then to the little back window, but all he could see was smoke. He felt as though the fire knew he was trapped. It was circling around him, the way that thing had stalked his brother. He heard its crackling footsteps and felt the heat rising inside the van.

Desperate to get out, Virgil kicked the silverware drawer out of his way and hurled the frying pan on top of it. He threw aside cushions and boxes and shoved the breadboard away. Right down at the bottom, he found his mother's favorite dish towel. Little blue sailboats bobbed on blue waves, the picture reminding Virgil of dinners round a picnic table. He pulled it free and wrapped the box inside it, tying the corners into a hobo's bundle.

From outside came the crash of a falling tree, the sudden splitting of wood, and a boom as it landed. With the box tucked under his arm, Virgil maneuvered around the seats and out through the windshield. The fallen tree lay across the road right in front of him.

In the few minutes he'd been inside the van, the fire had advanced a hundred yards. It had crossed the Boneyard behind him and blocked it in front, and in another ten minutes it would be all around him.

Virgil felt himself beginning to panic. Fear came in a little rush, grabbing hold of his body and mind. He wanted to run—it didn't matter where—just to escape from the fire. At the same time, he wanted to hide inside the van, to bury himself under all the debris, and wait for someone to help him. But he heard his mom's voice in his head, her old advice—"It's fear that will kill you"—and he forced himself to stop and think.

40

In the Darkness

Virgil remembered the sudden jolt that had sent Rusty careering off the road.

The washed-out culvert.

It was only a few yards away. He was there within seconds, scrambling down the little slope where the ditch had fallen away. The end of the culvert poked from the ground all rusted and bent. An old grate of welded rebar had been torn away and tossed aside, leaving the pipe wide open.

Virgil crawled inside.

It was cooler in there by twenty degrees and nearly as dark as night. Though only as long as the width of the road, it looked twice that length to Virgil. A small square of smoky daylight gleamed at the far end.

Virgil crawled deeper into the culvert. The metal felt cool under his hands and knees, and he had to work his way over tangles of sticks and branches that had washed into the pipe. When he could, he pushed the bundled box ahead of him, sliding it along the culvert. When he couldn't, he carried it in his teeth, biting down on the knot that he'd tied in the dish towel. In the middle he stopped, turned around, and lay flat on a narrow bed of dried mud.

He was pleased by the way things had turned out. If he hadn't forgotten the ashes, he would be bashing his way through the forest toward Little Lost Lake. Now, with the box tucked safely underneath him, he could let the fire sweep past over top of him. He thought he might get hot—maybe almost unbearably hot—but if he stayed where he was he'd be safe.

He could hear the fire coming. It seemed to be right at the end of the culvert behind him, trying to force its way in. In a moment, over the crackling of the fire, another sound echoed down the culvert.

A helicopter.

Virgil closed his eyes to listen. It was coming toward him, the fluttering noise of its rotors growing steadily louder.

He got up on his hands and knees and beetled toward the entrance. He crawled over the sticks and branches, over the hard ripples of the metal.

Virgil was halfway to the entrance when a shape appeared in the round mouth of the culvert. It looked like a cutout pasted onto the circle of light. But it turned and slipped into the pipe.

Virgil heard the helicopter hovering nearly above him. The steady beating of its blades vibrated through the culvert. He kept crawling toward the entrance, but carefully now. Whatever had come into the culvert was blocking his way.

"Kaitlyn?" he said hopefully. It was big enough to be her. Big enough, almost, to be a Sasquatch. But it didn't answer. It didn't move.

Virgil moved closer. He imagined the helicopter pilot looking down at the van, wondering if someone might be inside it. How long would he wait to find out?

With the bundle in his teeth, Virgil squirmed over a mass of sticks and grass. He saw the creature move, and its eyes suddenly gleamed, two little dots in the dark silhouette.

It snarled. A growl, a hiss, a quiet shriek; the sound was all those things at once. He had heard the same thing on the Boneyard when Joshua had said, "I think a mountain lion sounds like that." When the creature flashed a row of sharp, white teeth, Virgil knew his brother had been right. He had come face-to-face with a mountain lion.

It stood up and slinked toward him.

Virgil remembered his mother being suddenly afraid when she'd thought there was a mountain lion nearby.

– – –

He's walking with his mom down the trail to Little Lost Lake. They find scat on the ground, so fresh that it's steaming. A deerfly is crawling across it, twirling like a little dancer.

"Let's see what we're dealing with," says Mom. She crouches down and plucks a twig from a bush. She pokes at the scat, prying it apart, uncovering bits of bone and fur.

"Mountain lion," she says.

They have never seen a mountain lion at Little Lost Lake. Mom's surprised, and she seems frightened in a way that makes Virgil frightened too. Nervously, he says, "At least it's not a bear."

"Don't fool yourself," she tells him. "There's nothing more dangerous than a mountain lion."

She stands up slowly, looking into the bush. "I think we'll go back now," she says. "But carefully. If you see it, don't run. Don't make any sudden movements, and don't look into its eyes or it will think you're a threat. Just back away quietly, all right?"

He nods. But he doesn't feel reassured.

"Just remember; don't run," she says. "Never turn your back on a mountain lion."

– – –

Virgil crawled backward, deeper into the culvert. For every foot he moved back, the mountain lion moved a foot forward. Together they shuffled closer and closer to the little square of light that kept brightening behind Virgil.

The mountain lion hunched its back and lowered its head. It crept forward step-by-step, moving first a front leg then a hind leg. Its eyes never blinked, never turned aside.

Virgil couldn't see where he was going, and he didn't turn around to look. When he tangled his feet in a pile of branches and sprawled onto the culvert's floor, the mountain lion bounded toward him. It covered six feet in one leap, another six in a second, and crouched to leap again.

"No!" shouted Virgil.

It stopped and stared at him. Its tail swung slowly back and forth. It snarled that hiss and growl that made Virgil cold with fear.

The helicopter still hovered outside. Certain that it would leave at any moment, Virgil moved right back to the end of the culvert. He took a glance over his shoulder—just a glance—and saw a tangle of crisscrossing branches clogging the exit. In that moment, the mountain lion moved four feet toward him.

Virgil's shoulders were against the branches, and he couldn't go any farther. He turned around and started tearing them loose from the metal.

Through the first gap that he made, he saw the shadow of the helicopter cast onto the smoke like a giant dragonfly.

"Wait!" he screamed. "Don't leave!"

He pulled away another branch, not even looking back at the mountain lion. But through the next gap he made, Virgil saw a metal bar.

Behind the branches, the culvert was blocked by an iron grate welded to a hoop.

Virgil grabbed the bars and shook them. They rattled in their hoop with a clang that echoed through the culvert. When he looked over his shoulder he saw the mountain lion crouching, less than fifteen feet away.

"Go away!" he shouted. But the mountain lion didn't move. With its yellow eyes glaring, it pulled back its lips and let out that terrifying shriek that had come from the forest, that scream like a tortured woman's.

"No," said Virgil. "Please." He pressed himself back against the grate and yelled through the bars, hoping someone in the helicopter would hear him. "I'm in here. Help me!"

The mountain lion swished its tail. Its eyes narrowed, and its ears pulled back.

"Go away!" Virgil shouted again. He tore branches from the grate and hurled them at the mountain lion.

It lowered its head and crouched on the mud, ready to leap right at him.

41

A Flash of Orange

The helicopter tipped back and reeled across the road. Joshua looked down through the window as it tilted, and he saw Rusty lying on its side.

The grass at the side of the road was on fire. White smoke billowed over the Boneyard, hiding everything below.

With a flash of orange, the van exploded. The shock wave tossed the helicopter six feet higher and sent it spinning over the trees.

42

Down Here!

The explosion shook the grate. A rush of air blasted through the bars, hitting Virgil from behind. It slammed him face down in the mud.

It made the mountain lion turn and race away.

When Virgil looked up he saw it dashing down the culvert with its claws screeching on the metal. A streak of yellow with its tail between its legs, it leaped from the culvert and disappeared into the smoke.

Virgil grabbed his bundle and followed it. Like a hunched little gnome, he waddled down the pipe. With his ears ringing from the explosion, he couldn't hear the helicopter or anything else. He tumbled from the culvert, jumped to his feet, and flung his hands toward the sky.

"Down here!" he shouted. "I'm down here!"

He was half a minute too late. The helicopter was soaring up above the trees. In a moment, it was gone.

Just down the road, Rusty was a burning hulk. The tires were burning, the canvas was black and charred, and the roof was a splintered chunk of shattered fiberglass.

With the fire all around, Virgil had nowhere to go except back into the culvert or down the road. He thought of the mountain lion somewhere nearby, looking for its own place to hide. He imagined it coming back, trapping him inside the culvert. He could still get away from the fire, but what chance would he have with a hungry mountain lion?

"There's nothing more dangerous than a mountain lion."

Without another thought, Virgil started running. Past the burning van and on along the Boneyard, he ran for his life.

43

All Alone on the Boneyard

Virgil had never felt more alone. Smoke covered his world in a white fog and soaked up the sounds. The crunching of his shoes on the gravel sounded unnatural, and the blustery breath of the fire seemed to come from every direction.

He passed the sign for Mile 47 as the road curved downhill. Worried that the mountain lion might be stalking him, he walked right down the middle, watching the bushes on either side. But there seemed to be nothing alive in that world except for him. There were no birds to sing or chatter, no bugs to whine around his head. There were no shadows and there was no light, only the endless gray of the smoke, as thick as chowder. Tree branches loomed from the fog one after the other, shaggy arms reaching out to grab him.

Before he passed Mile 49, Virgil saw a sign for the Sasquatch museum. Below the silhouette of a shaggy, slouching

Sasquatch, the sign promised ice cream and frozen bait, "half a mile ahead."

The thought of ice cream made his mouth water. But Virgil thought he would walk right past the museum without stopping. He remembered his mother's fear of the place, her eerie inner sense that something awful would happen there.

But in that half mile, everything changed.

The smoke took on a thick, red glow. Virgil heard the fire storming through the forest behind him and felt himself on the edge of fear, wanting to run as fast as he could. He let himself jog, though the smoke made him cough as it thickened around him.

Soon he couldn't see from one side of the road to the other, so he kept close to the edge. When the skull of a bighorn sheep loomed beside him, staring back with gaping holes where the eyes had been, he knew he'd arrived at the Sasquatch museum.

The skull still had its long, curled horns attached. Pinned beside it were the leg bones, arranged in the X from a pirate's flag. Every ten feet there was another skull, or another arrangement of bones, all held to the fence with zip ties. As one faded behind, another appeared ahead.

Virgil remembered his mother's reaction the last time they drove past the museum, how she shivered at the sight of the skulls. The fog faded in his mind, replaced by a sunny day.

– – –

He's rolling down the Boneyard in Rusty, his whole family looking forward to a picnic at the lookout overseeing the Bigfoot River.

They know they're getting close to the Sasquatch museum. Joshua says, "Can we stop for ice cream?" He knows they won't, because they never do. He's asking just for a laugh.

Virgil's mom closes her eyes and covers them with her hands. "I'm not going to look," she says. "Tell me when we've passed it."

She does the same thing every year. But no matter how hard she tries, she can't stop herself from looking. She cracks her fingers apart, opens one eye, and peers at the skulls tied to the fence, at the things that hang from the trees.

It's like passing an accident with people still stuck in their cars. Dad can't help slowing the van and turning his head to gawk. Neither can Kaitlyn nor Joshua. Neither can Virgil, though looking makes him feel dirty somehow, as though he's seeing things he shouldn't be seeing.

"This place gives me the willies," says Mom. "I'm sure something bad will happen here."

"That's not very scientific," says Kaitlyn.

Mom agrees. "No, it's not. I can't explain it, but I know it's true."

- - -

Virgil could barely see the things in the trees. They hung far enough from the road that they might have been only shadows. But they gave him the same queasy feeling that he'd felt the first time he'd seen them, through Rusty's window years before. His dad had wondered why anyone would do a thing like that.

At the museum's driveway, a sign was nailed to a post.

ICE CREAM
PIZZA
FREE PARKING

When he saw it, Virgil slipped back to their very first trip down the Boneyard.

- - -

They've passed the skulls and the bones and the things in the trees, and they're all a bit shocked. When Joshua sees the sign, he points it out with a laugh.

"Hey, there's free parking, Dad," he says.

"Well, as tempting as that is," says Dad, "I don't think we'll stop here."

Mom isn't even smiling. She stares grimly at the sign as they pass it.

"In India there's an animal called the mugger crocodile," she says. "It lives in a pond surrounded by trees. In the springtime, when the birds begin nesting, it arranges sticks across its nose and lies in wait by the water. When the birds come gathering sticks, they find a nice selection at the crocodile's pond. But

when they land to get them, they get eaten instead. This place reminds me of that."

- - -

Through the smoke in the driveway, Virgil could just make out the ATCO trailer that housed the museum. He didn't want to go any closer, not with his mother's words fresh in his memory: "Something bad will happen here."

That was the only time she'd ever claimed to have a premonition. She had never believed in that sort of thing. But Virgil did, and he wondered if the terrible thing his mom had seen was about to happen right then.

He was scared—not just of the museum and the Bugaboo Man but of the fire coming behind him. He was thirsty and hungry and tired and sore, and it would be too hard to turn away and keep walking down the road. Virgil switched the bundled box to his left hand and started up the driveway.

He heard the purring of a generator as he reached the ATCO trailer. Up three wooden steps, he came to a little porch made of moldering wood. There was one window in the wall, with iron bars across the glass. A light was burning inside.

Virgil knocked on the door, but nobody answered.

He tried the handle. It turned easily, and the door swung open.

Inside was one big room, with a wooden Sasquatch standing on a platform covered with moss and river rock.

Carved by a chainsaw, from a single log, it was tall enough that the top of its head nearly touched the ceiling.

Display cases with glass tops were arranged along the walls. A set of shelves was stuffed with T-shirts and ball caps, and in the corner stood an ice cream cooler. The sight of it made Virgil drool.

"Hello," he shouted. Then again, louder. "HELLO?"

The cooler switched itself on with a click and a hum. The ceiling lights flickered, then brightened again as the sound of the generator murmured through the wall.

Virgil walked straight to the cooler and put his hands on the cold lid. Staring down through the glass, he saw one lonely looking Bomb Pop lying on a wire shelf.

He felt like a bird looking at the mugger crocodile's tempting sticks. But he couldn't stop himself from opening the lid. A thin cloud of cold air spilled from the cooler, frosting the glass.

Only once in his life had Virgil ever taken something without paying for it. He'd been in kindergarten then, and he had stolen a candy bar from the corner store. His dad had found out and had made him go back to pay for it. And apologize. "You can't steal from anyone without stealing from yourself," his dad had said. "You rob yourself of dignity."

Virgil looked over his shoulder. For a third time, he shouted hello. When nobody answered, he reached down and took the Bomb Pop.

He ate it right there, as fast as he could, without even bothering to close the cooler. He loved the cold, crunchy zing against his teeth, the icy thrill of each bite sliding down his throat. The Bomb Pop was gone in a moment, but Virgil's hunger was still there, aching in his stomach. Reaching down into the cooler, he broke off the film of frost and ice at the bottom and ate that as well.

Only then did he close the lid and look around the museum. He wandered along the row of display cases, barely stopping as he passed them. The first held a plaster casting of a big footprint, the second a clump of hair that might have been a dog's, the third a collection of blurry photographs. As he leaned on the glass to study them, he heard rain patter heavily against the trailer.

It was the nicest sound that Virgil had ever heard, and it made him smile and sigh. Hoping to soak himself in a downpour, he ran outside. But the smoky air looked as hot and dry as ever. It wasn't raining at all.

This made no sense to Virgil until he walked around the back of the trailer. A mobile home sat in a sea of junk, with a radio antenna poking up above the roof and an old Dodge truck parked beside it. Sitting on the open tailgate was a man as round as Humpty Dumpty. He had a huge, round belly, no neck at all, and skinny little legs sticking out from a pair of shorts. He was spraying the ATCO trailer with water from a garden hose, and he was drinking Mountain Dew from a plastic bottle. A half-empty case sat beside him.

He didn't look very scary for a Bugaboo Man. He was wearing a baseball cap—the same as the ones in the museum—and a colorful T-shirt that his made his belly look like a beach ball balanced on his lap. A pair of yellow flip-flops dangled from his tiny feet.

The water spewing from the hose made a glistening rainbow as it drummed on the roof. Virgil wanted nothing more than to stand in that spray and get wet, to drink till he couldn't drink any more.

The man turned his head and looked right at Virgil. "What are you doing here?" he asked. "Don't you know there's a fire coming, you dumb kid?"

"I'm trying to get away from it," said Virgil. "I was hoping you could help me."

"Maybe." The man looked slowly down to Virgil's feet and slowly up again, as though measuring him. "Yeah, I think I can help you."

"Do you have a telephone?"

"Nope. Phones don't work down here."

"A radio?"

The man shook his head.

Virgil nodded toward the mobile home. "You've got an antenna."

"It's busted."

"How can an antenna get busted?" asked Virgil.

"I mean the radio, dummy."

Virgil wondered what sort of help the man could give him. "Can you drive me out in the truck?" he asked.

"Nope."

"Why not?"

"Busted."

It seemed that everything the man owned was busted. But the generator kept humming away, powering the water pump and the ice-cream cooler that now sat empty in the

ATCO trailer. Virgil felt the same unease that his mother had talked about.

The man was watching him. Every time he breathed, his lip fluttered back, showing his teeth. Virgil decided to keep going to Little Lost Lake. But, first, he craved water.

"Can I have a drink?" he asked.

The man tossed the hose at Virgil's feet. It writhed like a green snake, hissing water from the nozzle. Virgil caught it by its head and took a long drink that tasted of rubber. But to Virgil it seemed delicious.

"Wet your shirt," said the man.

"Why?" asked Virgil.

"It lets you breathe." The man pulled the collar of his T-shirt wide open. He ducked his mouth inside it.

Virgil understood right away. The wet shirt would do more than filter the smoke. It would make an oxygen mask as the water evaporated. Virgil drenched his shirt, and when he pulled it over his mouth he breathed clearly and deeply for the first time that day.

The man held out his hand. "Give me back the hose."

Virgil hesitated. What if the man grabbed his hand instead of the hose? As fat as he was, he looked powerfully strong.

"Bring it here," said the man, waggling his fingers.

But Virgil didn't move any closer. He threw it onto the tailgate, and it landed across the man's legs.

As it slithered away, the man had to scramble to catch it. He aimed the spray of water at the wall, playing it from side to side. "So what's in the bundle?" he asked.

Virgil tightened his arm around the wooden box. "My mother's ashes."

"Show me."

Virgil opened the bundle just enough to uncover the wooden box.

The man grunted. "So why are you lugging your mother's ashes around in a burning forest?"

"We were taking them to Little Lost Lake," said Virgil. "Then our van broke down and we—"

"Who's 'we'?"

"My brother and sister and me."

"So where are they?"

"My brother went for help," said Virgil. Then he added quickly, "My sister's right behind me."

The man looked off toward the road, then back at Virgil. His eyes were puffy, ringed with folds of fat. Whenever he breathed, his lip curled back, showing his teeth. "Now I don't think you're telling the truth," he said. "I think you got separated somehow, and nobody knows where you are."

"We're supposed to meet up," said Virgil.

"Yeah. Down at the lake, I'm guessing."

Virgil fiddled with the towel that wrapped up the box. He was afraid the man could see through his eyes and know what he was thinking. "I'm going to keep going," he said.

"To the lake?"

"Yeah."

"You won't make it," said the man. "Not with this fire. She's going to burn up the whole valley."

"Then why are you still here?" asked Virgil.

"It's my home. It's all I got." The man gestured at the rundown trailer and the piles of junk. "The National Guard came to get me in a helicopter. I told them, I'm not leaving. I'm going to fight it, I said. They said okay, but you're on your own."

"What are you going to do?" asked Virgil.

"I'm doing it." The man played the water across the wall and up on the roof again. "I'll soak it down till the fire comes. Then I'll sit inside and wait her out."

Virgil had seen the forest burning and the van exploding, and he didn't believe the plan would work. "I don't think you can help me," he said. "I'm going to the lake."

"No. Wait," said the man. "I'll show you something."

He shut off the water and put down the hose. Then he wriggled to the end of the tailgate. "Ya want ice cream?"

"You mean the stuff in the cooler?" asked Virgil. "I took it."

"All of it?"

"Just a Bomb Pop," said Virgil. "That's all there was. Honest."

The man smiled. It was the most gruesome smile that Virgil had ever seen, full of teeth as jagged as the crocodile's. "Ya want some pop?"

"Sure. Thanks," said Virgil.

The box had been ripped open, torn apart as though by a pack of wolves. The man pushed it closer. "Take two."

Virgil did, but as warily as a squirrel at a bird feeder. He stuffed one bottle into his bundle and opened the other. Mountain Dew fizzed out in a hot fountain, and the man smiled his slimy, crocodile smile.

Virgil capped the bottle and slipped it into the bundle as well. As he tightened the knot, a snowstorm of ash started falling. Huge gray flakes floated down from the smoke. They reminded Virgil of shredded scraps from a beehive, and they fell in slow spirals. Virgil held out his hand and watched them pile on his palm.

"She's coming faster now," said the man. "Half an hour, she'll be here."

"Then I'd better go," said Virgil.

"No," said the man again. "I said I got something to show you."

"What is it?"

"Well, come and see."

The man's flip-flops slapped against his feet as he hopped down from the tailgate. Virgil followed him down a path beside the mobile home. The backs of his thighs were marked with red and white stripes from sitting on the metal.

Already a quarter-inch deep on the ground, the ash kept falling. It covered the man's hair and lay thickly on his shoulders. He said, "I've got a safe place for you back here."

"Where?" asked Virgil.

"You'll see."

Virgil walked in the man's footprints, past a pile of old tires and a pyramid of rusted propane tanks. There was a stack of lumber that bristled with nails, and then a garden where mounds of earth lay overgrown with weeds.

The man led Virgil through the rubble to a thing that looked like a giant beehive. It was a mound of mud on a platform made of bricks, with a little metal door locked by an iron bar. The man heaved up the bar and swung the door open. It screeched on its hinges.

"Get inside," he said.

Virgil gaped. The opening was so narrow that he would have to squeeze himself through it.

"Go on, get in," said the man. "You'll be safe in there."

"What is it?" asked Virgil.

"What does it look like? It's a pizza oven."

Virgil stepped back. There was no chance he would crawl into that darkness. He imagined the man slamming the door behind him and dropping the bar into place. It was the craziest thing he'd ever been asked to do, to crawl inside an oven.

"Well, what are you waiting for?" The man smiled through the falling ash. "That's the safest place in the valley. There's three inches of mud with brick underneath it. Mud don't burn, boy, no matter how hot it gets."

Virgil peered into the oven. The floor was covered with old ash and bits of black charcoal.

"Get in," said the man again.

"You'll lock me inside," said Virgil.

"You dumb kid. That's a monster coming," said the man. "This is your only chance. I'd get in there myself if I could."

Above the ATCO trailer, a deep-red glow pulsed through

the smoke. The flakes of ash tumbled down onto the piles of junk and the rounded roof of the oven.

"I'm not wasting anymore time with you," said the man. "An hour from now, everything here is going to be gone. It will go up like kindling, the whole damn works. That's the only safe place in the valley, inside that oven."

Virgil thought the man could be right. Too big to fit into the oven himself, maybe he really was offering a way to survive. But Virgil felt the strange, tingling feeling his mom used to feel. She had taught him to fear the Bugaboo Man, to be afraid of his place and everything in it.

"Get in!" said the man.

Virgil stood there with his bundle and couldn't decide what to do. The man wasn't smiling anymore. When his lip fluttered again, he looked like the mountain lion snarling in the culvert. Every bit as fast as the big cat, he reached out and grabbed Virgil's arm.

"Let me go!" Virgil tried to pull away.

But the man was stronger. His other hand clamped around Virgil's neck. He pushed him toward the oven door.

Virgil twisted and squirmed, trying to get free. He kicked the man's leg as hard as he could, and when his hand loosened around his neck he whirled away. The man tried to grab him again but clutched the bundle instead. A bottle fell out. The man ignored it and tossed the bundle through the oven door.

It slid right to the back of the oven.

"Go get it," said the man.

Virgil didn't move.

"I'm trying to help you!"

For a moment, Virgil believed him. The man had given him water and pop. He'd offered him ice cream. There was no reason *not* to trust him. But Virgil remembered his mother's warning: "I wouldn't go inside that place for all the money in the world." He might be able to ignore his own strange feelings, but certainly not his mother's.

"Can I get my pop?" he asked.

"Sure." The man gave the bottle a kick, sending it spinning a little closer.

Virgil bent over and picked it up. With his head down, he charged forward, driving his shoulder into the man's bulging stomach.

With a cry, the man staggered back.

Virgil had never hit anybody. But in that moment he was the big, tough kid he'd always wanted to be. He threw himself at the man with his fists swinging wildly. The man took quick shuffling steps as he tried to keep his balance. With his arms held out, he fell over backward. The cap flew from his head. One of his flip-flops sprang away. He fell as stiff as a falling plank, like a child making snow angels, and the ash puffed up all around him.

Virgil leaped up to the oven. As he crawled through the door he blocked the light, and he had to grope across the floor to find his bundle.

44

Air Tankers

The Beast had again doubled in size. Spread across twenty thousand acres, it filled the sky with so much smoke that people five thousand miles away saw an orange moon in their night sky.

Flames soared hundreds of feet into the air, and the temperature inside the fire reached more than a thousand degrees.

Far from its leading edge, firefighters dug in for a battle. Bulldozers scraped away the forest in a desperate attempt to stop the Beast. With no rain in the forecast, they had only one way to slow it down. They called in the water bombers.

Twin-engine planes with tanks full of water, they were guided over the fire by little Cessnas. A hundred feet above the trees, they bombed the Beast with a ton of water at a time.

45

You Have to Be Lucky

Virgil backed out of the oven. With his bottle in one hand and the bundle in the other, he ran past the museum and out to the Boneyard, along the fence with the crucified birds. Afraid that the man had lied about the truck and was already racing after him, Virgil abandoned the road and fled through the forest.

He ran until he was out of breath. Surrounded by trees, he stopped and took a moment to decide which way to go. Then he headed off, hoping to find his way to Little Lost Lake.

Though he was heading away from the fire, the sound of its breath grew steadily louder behind him. The smoke kept thickening around him, hiding the trees he needed for guideposts. His bundle kept snagging on bushes and twigs, ripping the threads from his mother's towel. The blue waves unraveled; the sailboats shredded apart. Soon all he had was a tattered rag that flapped behind him as he moved through the forest.

In Rusty, it would take fifteen minutes to drive from the Sasquatch museum to the pullout where they would first see the Bigfoot River. Dad stopped there every year. Sometimes he would get out his sketchbook, and they would have to wait while he drew the distant Bigfoot winding through its canyons. There was a waterfall there, and a whirlpool that never stopped turning. Virgil remembered his mom telling him that river rafters called the white spiral of water "the slaughterhouse."

He slipped back to that day with her words in his mind.

– – –

Six years old again, he's watching two canoes floating down the Bigfoot River. From the viewpoint, they look about as big as grains of rice. The paddlers, two in each boat, are just orange specks in their bright life jackets.

"They must be crazy," says Dad.

He's standing beside Rusty, eating a tuna sandwich. The river is at least a thousand feet below them and more than a mile away. A dotted line through the valley, it appears only here and there, in canyons and gorges. Its bright blue water is streaked with foam.

The canoes are drifting along at the speed of the river. They're just above a stretch of rapids called the gun barrel.

"They'll be lucky if they make it," says Dad.

"Oh, they won't run the rapids," says Mom. She's been down

the whole river in kayaks and rafts; she knows what it's like. "They'll land above the gorge and portage round the falls."

A quarter mile above the gorge, the river is calm and shot with sunlight. Carried along by the current, the canoes move a little faster.

Virgil feels a growing dread as the tiny boats are swept on by the Bigfoot. Soon they'll start through the big bend. The river will turn twice in an S shape and squeeze itself through the narrow canyon of the gun barrel. But the biggest dangers will still be ahead: a waterfall twenty feet high and the whirlpool of the slaughterhouse.

The canoes are floating along in the middle of the stream. But if they don't head for shore in the next five minutes, it will be too late. They'll be sucked into the gun barrel and over the falls.

"I wonder if we can signal," says Dad. "Virgil, honk the horn."

Virgil climbs into Rusty's front seat. He presses the horn and hears that sad little bleep, one long note.

The sound echoes back from the mountains. But the canoes keep moving along.

"Again," says Dad.

Virgil blasts out the SOS that he learned from his mom: three short beeps, three longer ones, three short ones again.

The canoes keep drifting. They start round the first turn of the S and disappear into the gorge.

Virgil honks his SOS again.

And then they wait.

The river tumbles along. Virgil can actually hear it going over the falls, a quiet thundering sound that makes him think of surf on a sandy beach.

Five minutes go by and there's no sign of the canoes.

"They must have landed in the canyon," says Dad.

But Mom doesn't believe it. "The walls are a hundred feet high and they're as smooth as glass. A spider couldn't climb them."

Just then one of the canoes comes rushing from the gorge. It's sideways to the current, the people paddling frantically to straighten it out. The other appears a moment later, its tiny hull there and gone and there again as water rolls right over it.

They tip over the falls. One vanishes and never comes up again, and the other comes up in the slaughterhouse. Four orange specks spin along with it, and the whirlpool carries them up to the falls and around again.

It spits out two of them; it spits out another, and one orange speck keeps twirling round and round in that spiral of white water.

"He looks like a spider going down a drain," says Joshua.

Virgil had been thinking the same thing but didn't want to say it. Up close, he imagined, the person in the river would look exactly the same as a spider, arms flailing in a mindless terror.

Somehow the four paddlers survive. They gather driftwood for a campfire on the shore. The smoke drifts along the water, up toward the gorge.

"We can all learn something from this," says Mom. "If you come into this land unprepared, you have to be lucky to get out alive."

- - -

Virgil forced himself out of the memory. Desperate to stay ahead of the fire, he pushed himself on. But he couldn't tell anymore where it was. Wherever he looked, the smoke was the same blur of orange and gray. His only hope was to keep going between the Boneyard and the river. The forest that he'd feared so much was now his safety zone.

If he veered too far and reached the river, he would find himself trapped above the canyon with the fire sweeping toward him. If that ever happened he would be faced with an unthinkable choice: to burn up in the fire or to tackle those cliffs that a spider couldn't climb. He would have to cling to little bits of rock on a skyscraper wall high above the water. The thought was so frightening that he knew he could never do it.

The trees he lined up were closer together all the time. He listened for the sound of the river and picked a few berries as he walked along. But it was just as Kaitlyn had said; they were hard and shrunken, and he spat more of them out than he swallowed.

At an enormous fallen tree, Virgil stopped for a drink of Mountain Dew. He told himself he'd have just one sip, but once he started he couldn't stop, and he ended up drinking a third of the bottle. Then he wrapped it into his ragged bundle and examined the tree in front of him.

It must have been a giant standing up. Now, as it lay on the ground, Virgil couldn't see over the top of it. But he couldn't get underneath it, and he didn't want to waste the time it would take to walk all the way around it. So he went straight up, tearing handfuls from the moss that covered the tree, kicking away chunks of rotten bark. When his hand plunged into a nest of termites he felt sick with disgust and loathing.

There might have been a thousand of them in the hollow he'd uncovered. Their pale bodies felt soft and bloated, and he hated the feeling of them squirming between his fingers. When he pulled out his hand, he saw a dozen clinging to his skin, and he shook them off with a frantic twitch.

It reminded him of a day years before at Little Lost Lake.

— — —

He's a little boy once more. Mom has walked into the camp with a big smile on her face.

"Anyone want to eat a bug?" she asks.

She's carrying the plastic pot that she uses for berry picking. She puts it down on Rusty's step and sits beside it.

"I found them under a rock," she says. "Come look."

Virgil doesn't really believe her. He walks over, expecting to see a collection of huckleberries and thimbleberries. But instead he finds a horde of grubs.

They're each about half an inch long, round and plump, with eyes at one end and tiny feet kicking at the other. They cover the bottom of the pot in a writhing mass, but some are climbing the sides and are nearly at the top. Mom shakes the pot to knock them down again.

Kaitlyn and Joshua have the same reaction when they look in the pot. So does Dad. They all look disgusted. They cry, "Eww!" and "Ughh!"

Mom laughs. "All over the world, people eat insects," she says. "I think we should give it a try."

"Not me." Dad holds up his hands in his surrendering gesture.

Beside him, Joshua does the same thing. "No, thanks," he says.

Kaitlyn is more blunt. "You're sick, Mom."

But Virgil is curious. "Are you really going to eat them?"

"I'll try them," says Mom. "Why not?"

She picks a twig from the ground and sticks it into the pot. "If everyone ate insects it could end starvation," she says. "They're very nutritious, you know."

Three grubs are holding onto the stick when she pulls it out. They squirm and wriggle.

Dad has wandered far away, but Kaitlyn and Joshua are watching closely. Kaitlyn says, "Mom, if you eat those I'll throw up."

"I think we should all try them," says Mom. "Who knows, you might find yourself lost in the woods one day. If you know you can eat grubs, you won't have to worry about food. These are everywhere."

She plucks one of the grubs from the twig. Pinched between her fingers, it wriggles and twists as though trying to escape, as though it knows it's about to be eaten. Mom moves it toward her mouth.

Then she laughs and flings the grub away. "No, I can't do it," she says, and shakes like a wet dog.

She takes the pot a few yards from the van and empties it into the bushes.

"I wonder why that is, why we find grubs and larvae so disgusting," she says. "It doesn't make any sense really."

"Maybe it's 'cause they're disgusting," says Kaitlyn.

"But why?" Mom puts down the empty pot. It will be a week before anyone will eat berries out of it again.

"People say they're delicious. But I guess we'll never know."

As he stared into the nest of termites, Virgil felt the same squeamishness he'd felt that day as he'd waited for his mom to eat the grubs. It was thinking about eating them that was really disgusting.

He was painfully hungry. In two days, all he'd eaten was a few spoonfuls of soup and a Bomb Pop. But the squirming mass of termites still sickened him. He imagined them writhing in his stomach, trying to crawl back up his throat, and wondered if he could even keep them down.

If they were dead, it would be easier. But he wasn't going to bonk each one on its tiny head. If he was going to eat them, he would have to eat them alive.

Virgil couldn't bear to plunge his hand into that squishy mass of bugs again. So he did what his mom had done: broke a twig from a branch and poked it among them.

He didn't wait for the termites to grab onto the stick. He stabbed at the nest, again and again, piercing the fat bodies until he had a sickening kebab of squirming bugs.

Without stopping to think about it, he stuck the twig into his mouth and pulled off the termites against his teeth.

He felt them fall onto his tongue. They wriggled against his gums and down his throat as he swallowed. For a moment he was sure he would throw up, and he leaned forward, ready to vomit onto the moss. But the feeling passed, and he stabbed again at the nest.

The bugs weren't delicious. Virgil didn't even taste them. He filled his mouth and swallowed without chewing, just eating to stop from being hungry. When he was finished, he threw away the twig. He emptied the first bottle of pop, but couldn't bring himself to toss that away too. He would have felt too guilty. If we don't look after the forest it won't look after us, his mother had told him.

Virgil tied both bottles into the bundle. He burped, tasting soda pop and termites, then scrambled across the log and went on toward the river.

It was about half an hour later when he found a trail trampled through the bushes. Broken twigs and torn-away leaves showed that someone or something had passed by only a few minutes earlier. The leaves were still green and stiff. They hadn't had time to yellow.

It didn't take Virgil very long to figure out which way the person or creature had been walking. The broken twigs and pushed-aside branches were all bent in the same direction.

Virgil put his hands to his mouth to shout for help. But he wondered who—or what—would hear him, and lowered his hands without making a sound. He pushed the branches apart and followed whatever had gone before him.

46

At the Cliff

The trail was not hard to follow. But it kept turning to one side or another, never going straight for more than a few yards at a time. It had been made in a hurry.

Virgil was afraid he was following a Sasquatch, or maybe the Bugaboo Man trying to follow *him*. But he didn't think it was likely. The trail was too narrow for the fat man and not tall enough for a Sasquatch. Virgil couldn't see any broken twigs or torn leaves any higher above the ground than his own shoulders.

He went as fast as he could down the wobbling trail, wondering where it would take him. He kept peering ahead between the trees, looking for a figure hurrying along. In a patch of currants, he found long threads tangled among the leaves. With a feeling of dread he pulled them free.

They matched the ones in his unraveling towel.

He was following his own trail.

That was a big disappointment and an even bigger worry. Though he had carefully kept the trees in line as his mother had taught him to do, he had gone in a circle. And now he had no idea where he was or which way he was supposed to go.

He turned round and round, listening for the fire, looking for its glow in the smoke. But the sound seemed all around him, and the colors were all the same.

Virgil felt the panic his mother had warned him about. It filled him in an instant with the urge to start running. But he remembered her warning: "It's fear that will kill you." And again he forced himself to stop and think.

"Moss keeps out of the sun. Spiders keep out of the wind."

His mother had taught him that as well, showing him how he could find his way by looking at spiderwebs and moss on the trees. But she had warned him not to rely too much on that.

"Your spider might not have read the rule book," she'd said.

But Virgil didn't have a choice. He had to keep moving. He had to find his way to Little Lost Lake before the fire caught him.

Virgil walked slowly through the forest, looking for moss and spiderwebs. In a few moments he saw that his problem wasn't how to find them. It was finding too many of them. Every tree had moss on every side, and nearly every bush held a spiderweb. They were low to the ground and high in the trees. They were out in the open and deep in the bushes. There were webs that were big and flimsy, and webs that were small and thick. But Virgil looked only for those that were speckled with needles and leaves. Some were covered almost completely.

Virgil noticed that and smiled.

The answer to his problem lay right in front of him, and it had been there all along. He was looking down at a natural compass.

"It has the most beautiful name of all," his mom had said. "We call it 'katabatic.' "

Virgil remembered exactly when she had taught him that. In his mind he was back at the lookout above the Bigfoot River, on the day the canoes had gone over the waterfall.

- - -

The smoke from the paddlers' campfire floats above the river, stretching out toward the falls. Like so many things he notices, it makes Virgil curious.

"Does the wind always blow along a river?" he asks.

Kaitlyn rolls her eyes. "Who cares? Can we go now?"

She wants to get back in the van, to get down to Little Lost Lake. Everything's always a hurry for Kaitlyn.

"I'm just wondering," says Virgil. He has spent a lot of time sitting beside little rivers, watching his mom fishing for trout with her fly rod. He loves to watch her line curve through the air as it whips the little fly out into the current. He has seen it bending in the wind, up the river and down the river, but

never right back toward her. "Mom, does the wind ever blow across the river?"

"I wouldn't say never," says Mom. "But not usually."

"Why?"

"A river valley is like a big funnel," she says. "Air moves through it according to the time of day. Upstream in the afternoon. Downstream in the morning."

Despite herself, Kaitlyn has become interested. "Why does the time make a difference?" she asks.

"Because air warms up in the daytime," says Mom. "As it gets hot it rises up through the valley. When it starts to cool in the evening, the flow reverses. An upriver wind is called 'anabatic.'"

"What do you call a downriver wind?" asks Virgil.

"Oh, it has the most beautiful name of all," says Mom. "We call it 'katabatic.'"

– – –

Virgil looked at the spiderwebs and thought of the wind blowing up and down the valley. It had shaken the tiniest twigs from the bushes and blown them through the forest. The webs that had snared the most debris had to be hanging across the wind, and so, across the valley. The ones that were empty lay in line with the anabatic wind, showing the way to Little Lost Lake.

But when he started walking, Virgil couldn't be sure if he was heading toward Little Lost Lake or off in the opposite direction. The ground was uneven, the smoke too thick to let him see very far. There were places where he walked uphill, and places where he walked down, but he felt he was going more down than up, and that was the way he wanted to go.

As he walked along, Virgil started chanting. "Anabatic. Katabatic." He said the words over and over, again and again, until they became a blur without meaning. *Katabaticanabatic.* He put a little tune behind them and walked through the forest singing.

But he stopped when he heard an engine growling in the smoke.

The sound grew louder by the moment. But it seemed to come from everywhere at once, a bubble of noise all around him.

He looked up, trying to see through the tangled branches. Almost right above him, an enormous airplane hurtled through the smoke. By the time he could turn around to watch it go, it was already out of sight.

But another was coming behind it.

Virgil started running. He bounded through the forest with the bundle bouncing in his arms, trying to reach a clearing before the airplane roared above him. He could see one up ahead, a patch of moss and yellow grass.

But he didn't quite make it.

Just as he reached the edge of the clearing, the airplane passed overhead. It was an air tanker, a Bombardier 415. He had watched one working in Idaho, skimming across the surface of a mountain lake to fill its enormous belly. The growl of its engines as it labored into the sky had been such a thrilling sound that his dad had written a poem about it.

From the edge of the clearing, Virgil watched the plane fade away into the smoke. Though he knew it was useless, he yelled at the pilot to stop and come back. He yelled just for the sake of yelling, because there was nothing else he could do.

When the sound of the planes had faded away, Virgil opened his bundle and took a drink of Mountain Dew. He swished it around his mouth and between his teeth before he swallowed it. Then, with a sigh, he packed up the bottle and turned to follow the air tankers. If they came back the same way, he would signal to the pilots and hope they'd see him. But even if they didn't—even if they had no idea they were helping him—they would lead him to a lake big enough to let a Bombardier fill its tank, maybe even Little Lost Lake itself.

Up a little slope and down the other side, through tangled boxwood and Oregon grape, Virgil kept trudging along. His feet were sore, his knees hurt, and he wished he could lie down for a sleep. But the fire was coming behind him.

When he heard the planes heading back to wherever they'd come from, Virgil was sure he would soon be saved. He would reach the lake and stand on its shore, waving his arms till the pilots saw him. It couldn't be far away. He watched through the trees for the gleam of water and imagined what he would do when he got there.

He wouldn't stop, that was for sure. He would just keep walking, over the shore and into the cold water. It would rise over his ankles, over his knees, but he wouldn't stop until he was floating. Then he would drift on his back, looking up at the sky as he waited for the planes to return.

But instead of a lake, he found flames.

They gleamed through the smoke, writhing and tossing, leaping high from the ground. They shone red and yellow, orange and white, changing shape all the time. They were beautiful but terrifying.

In that moment, Virgil believed he was surrounded by fire. The forest had been burning behind him, and now it had somehow leaped ahead of him. Again he felt himself starting to panic, and again he fought it down.

When he sat down and thought about it calmly, everything made sense. The planes were flying low because they were heading for the fire with a full load of water. When they went back empty, they climbed above the smoke, too high for him to see. He had been following them away from the lake instead of toward it. The fire was not all around him.

When Virgil stood up and started walking, he knew for sure that he was going in the right direction. But the fire was moving faster. He saw flames leaping along on one side and then on the other. They bounded from tree to tree as though trying to circle ahead of him. When he found a dried-up stream, he turned to run beside it.

He remembered the lesson he'd learned as a child.

– – –

His mom is sending him off to the lake by himself, the first time she's ever done that. He's only going to the bluff above the lake; he'll be there in twenty minutes. But she makes him feel like Meriwether Lewis heading out across America.

"Stay on the trail," she tells him. "Remember to take the right fork going there and the left fork coming back."

Around his neck she hangs an orange whistle on a green string. "If you get lost, signal for help. You remember the SOS?"

"Yes, Mom."

"Three dots, three dashes, three dots again."

"Yes, Mom," he says. "I remember."

"If you somehow get off the trail and think you're lost, don't keep wandering around. Sit down and signal your SOS and wait for someone to come and get you. All right?"

"Yes, Mom."

"But if something goes wrong and nobody comes, the best thing to do is follow a stream. It doesn't matter how big it is, because it will always flow into something bigger. Understand? Always follow the water."

"Yes, Mom."

She makes sure that his shoes are tied. Then she stands up and pats his shoulder. "Now go and have fun."

– – –

The sound of the air tankers brought Virgil out of his memory. He looked up and turned around, trying to see where they were coming from. Even lower than before, they thundered across the forest and passed him in a blink.

Through a cockpit window, Virgil saw the pilot's helmet and sunglasses. Such a tiny figure running that huge machine, thought Virgil. He was a dinosaur's brain.

Virgil didn't wait to watch them disappear. With the fire

racing him on either side, he jumped back and forth across the stream bed to avoid the fallen trees. In places he ran right down the middle of it, his feet crunching on brittle leaves and fir cones.

"It will always flow into something bigger."

Virgil imagined the stream becoming a river, stretching out a mile wide. He saw himself running beside it past farmyards and cities, over prairie and mountains, arriving at last at the ocean.

He never dreamed that the stream might end. But it did, suddenly, at the edge of a cliff. Panting for breath, he stood looking straight down.

It wasn't the Bigfoot River below him. The cliff that blocked his way seemed small compared to the terrifying thing that walled in the river. But it was still fifty feet high, too steep to let him climb down. He was trapped all the same.

There were flames to his left and flames to his right. The choice that he'd found too horrible to think about was suddenly unavoidable. Would he burn up in the fire, or would he tackle the cliff?

47

Over the Edge

Virgil watched the flames moving toward him. They were like wolves closing in for a kill, coming at him turn by turn instead of all in a rush. As he looked toward one, another crept forward, and the whole ring slowly tightened around him.

He crouched there on the dried-up streambed, a foot from the edge, and hoped the fire wouldn't reach him.

The heat was unbelievable. Virgil had stood at Uncle Birdy's forge, feeding metal sheets of flame that blasted from the burners. He had worn heavy gloves and a leather apron and still felt as though he'd melt in the heat. But compared to the burning forest, his uncle's forge might have been a refrigerator.

Burning sticks popped from the flames and shot toward him. They whirled up into the smoke and came tumbling down through the trees.

Virgil backed right to the edge. With his eyes watering, he could see nothing below him but clouds of smoke.

The sound of the fire filled his ears. The heat scorched his skin. He pulled out the last bottle of Mountain Dew and poured some over his shirt to let him breathe. Then he tore the towel, tied a loop, and hung his bundle around his neck. Lying flat on the rock, he wriggled back until his stomach pressed against the edge and his legs dangled free.

He danced his feet along the rock, feeling for a nubbin of stone or a ledge he could stand on. But his feet swung through the air, and the fire moved closer.

Virgil pushed himself back until he nearly teetered over the edge. When his toes stubbed against something hard, he couldn't wait to figure out what it was. He loosened his grip on the rock and let himself slither over the cliff.

It was the root of an ancient tree that took his weight and held him up. Black and scaly, it sprouted from the cliff in elaborate curves. It was no thicker than a rolling pin, and all but a few inches had broken away.

It bent underneath him, prying pebbles from the cliff. They tumbled away into the smoke.

Virgil ducked his head below the edge of the cliff. The smoke billowed above him, and he looked down through gray mist to the forest below.

Water pouring over the cliff had carved a hollow at the bottom, now dry and filled with pine cones, needles, and branches. From there, the dead stream wound away between the trees, through a clearing that once had been a pond or a tiny lake. Grass grew tall and yellow there.

Virgil pressed himself against the cliff, clinging to the rock by his fingertips. The smoke rolled along above him, over the cliff, and on across the forest. Trees exploded into flames with the sounds of rockets blasting.

Shielded from the heat and the smoke, Virgil thought he could hold on until the fire burned its way past him. Then he would climb up and make his way through a smoldering, ruined forest to wherever he wanted to go. Back to the Boneyard or down to the lake, it wouldn't matter. There would be nothing that could hurt him anymore.

When he heard the air tankers coming, he looked up. And his hope vanished.

Right above Virgil's head, a burning tree hung over the cliff. Flames encircled the trunk, climbing toward the branches. When it fell over—and it *had* to fall over—it would land right on top of him.

Virgil tried to scramble across the cliff. But there were no handholds nearby, only a split in the rock a little farther away than he could reach. He leaned sideways, stretching his fingers toward it. The old root that he stood on shifted under his weight.

Spread-eagled across the cliff, Virgil hooked one finger into the cracked rock. A clump of smoldering leaves fell past his head, streaming curls of smoke. A twig landed on his wrist and burst into tiny embers. When he moved his arm to shake it away, he lost his balance and began to topple sideways. He threw himself against the cliff, holding on by his fingernails.

With a snap, a branch broke loose from the tree. It

swung down on a hinge of bark, banging Virgil's shoulder. Then it swung the other way and snagged in the bundle that hung from his neck.

The old towel started smoldering. Little red eyes appeared, widening as the threads began to burn. Virgil tried to pull it free, and the bottle of Mountain Dew fell spinning down the cliff. The box of ashes followed it, bouncing off his foot, tumbling into the hollow below him.

With another crack, the branch tore from its hinge and hurtled past him. All its weight snapped tight on the towel, ripping through the threads, yanking Virgil from the cliff.

He tried to grab the rock. His hands scraped down the cliff, pulling away dirt and pebbles that skittered along with him. He reached out for the root he'd been standing on, and he caught it in the crook of his arm.

Fifteen feet above the ground, Virgil stopped falling. The root bent and groaned, but it held fast in the rock. Virgil kicked at the cliff until he found a tiny spot to wedge one foot. Looking down past his legs, he saw the wooden box with his mother's ashes lying in the hollow below him. The burning branch had landed a few feet away, and flames were spreading across the hollow toward the box.

Leave it, Virgil told himself. Let it burn; it's only a box. But he remembered his father handing it to Joshua for the trip to Little Lost Lake. He wouldn't release it until he was sure that Joshua was holding it firmly. Then he'd bent his head and given the box a kiss goodbye.

What was it that Joshua had said? "It's the most valuable thing we have."

Virgil let go of the root. He slithered down the cliff, grabbing stones and spikes of rock, trying to slow his fall. His bruised hip whacked against a rock, and with an awful thump he landed at the bottom and tumbled across the ground.

He thought he'd broken his leg. It throbbed from ankle to hip, so painful that he squeezed his fists and breathed in little gasps. But the pain eased off as he lay there, and nothing was broken or bleeding. He got up and snatched the box from the flames.

A hinge was missing. The hasp was bent. One corner was charred, and the nameplate was blackened, but the box was still mostly whole, the ashes still inside it.

The bottle of Mountain Dew was lying nearby, and Virgil took that as well. He turned around to limp away. But he had nowhere left to go.

The fire was spreading along the bottom of the cliff. It had leapfrogged over the treetops, and the forest was burning in front of him. His fear of being surrounded by flames had come true.

Right above him, at the edge of the cliff, the tree was leaning nearly ninety degrees, shedding branches and twigs and bundles of fire. Afraid it would come crashing down on top of him, Virgil shuffled off among the trees, into the clearing that had once been a pond.

He couldn't go any farther. Virgil stood in the smoke and held onto the box, wishing he had stayed at the Sasquatch museum. The worst thing of all was being so alone.

48

Hush Little Baby

In the middle of the clearing, waiting for the fire to close around him, Virgil thought of the Bugaboo Man. Had he really being trying to help? Had he really wanted to save him by shoving him into the oven? Would that huge beehive of brick and mud have kept him alive even if everything else went up in flames?

"Mud don't burn, boy," the man had said. "No matter how hot it gets."

That made Virgil think. It made him use that brain of his.

He dropped to his knees on the dry grass. He put down the box and the bottle of pop and started digging with his hands. He tore up the grass in big clumps and shoveled down with his fingers, into the earth where a pond had been in the rainy days of the year. Deeper and deeper, he worked his way down.

Almost a foot from the surface, his hands sank into soft, black mud.

He might survive, he thought, if he could bury himself in the ground.

Virgil limped back to the foot of the cliff and found a stout branch and a rock. With one for a pick and the other for a hammer, he scraped out a hollow that looked so much like a grave that he didn't want to think about getting inside it.

The heat made him feel faint. The smoke made him cough and wheeze. But he wouldn't let himself take a drink of Mountain Dew or use it to wet his shirt. There was so little left that he couldn't waste a drop.

The fire was all around him. It covered the ground and climbed through the trees. Virgil imagined it spreading across the clearing as he lay huddled under the ground, and he thought he was stupid for thinking he could live through it. If the flames didn't burn him up they would roast him alive as they roared through the grass.

But what if the grass was already burned? Would he be safe in the clearing then, surrounded by mud that couldn't burn?

Holding the box and the bottle to keep them safe, Virgil hobbled back toward the cliff and picked up a burning branch. He set fire to the clearing, touching the branch to the grass as he shuffled round the edge. The flames were so hot that they were almost invisible. As they moved across the clearing the grass seemed to turn from yellow to black, and a blanket of smoke rolled out ahead of them.

In less than a minute the clearing was a charred black

circle. Virgil drenched his shirt with the last of the Mountain Dew and pulled the collar over his nose. He kicked the smoldering grass from his hollow and crawled inside it with the box of ashes. Like a mole he tunneled deeper, scraping mud and dirt on top of himself.

Miles from the road and miles from the lake, all alone in the valley of the Bigfoot, Virgil buried himself and his box of ashes.

On every side of the old pond, flames spiraled up the trees. They twisted away in a wind that was growing stronger every moment. The towel flapped on the ground, then suddenly soared away into the smoke. The pop bottle stood up and bounded across the clearing. Leaves spun round and round in a whirlwind of fire.

Virgil felt the heat pressing down through the mud and the dirt. He wanted to spring up from his little grave and run away from the fire. But he forced himself to lie still. He held onto the box and cried for his mother.

Fire filled the forest for a mile all around. Virgil passed out, woke up, felt the dirt being lifted away from his back.

His mother was there. He saw her smiling down at him through a hole in the dirt. He felt her fingers, soft and cool, brush against his forehead, and he heard her whispering a lullaby.

In his mind, the flames disappeared. He was no longer lying alone in a burning forest. He was a child again, safe in his own bedroom.

– – –

He has a fever. His mother is sitting at the side of the bed with a bowl of cool water. She covers his forehead with a damp cloth, holds his hand, and smiles. She tries to sing him to sleep.

"Hush little baby, don't you cry."

In a whispering voice she sings about all the many things she will buy for him. They parade through his feverish mind, whirling across the room: a mockingbird and a looking glass, a diamond ring and a billy goat that gambols across his bureau.

He falls asleep and has terrible dreams, and when he wakes, she's still there.

She feeds him chicken soup with big, fat noodles. She keeps touching his hair, touching his face, smiling with her eyes so bright and shiny.

It's dark outside, and she's there. It's daylight again, and she's there.

"Hush little baby," she sings. "Don't you cry."

- - -

Virgil woke up. He felt the blistering heat of the fire, and the sound thrummed in his ears, as though he were lying under water.

The dirt he'd pulled into the hollow was shifting in front of him. Dust floated up into the sky, sucked by the wind that whirled through the clearing. Tiny pebbles spun round and round, then skittered out over the edges.

The wooden box began to shake in the cradle of his arms.

Virgil held it tightly. The broken hinge rattled against

the wood. The battered corner split apart, and the ashes gushed out in a gray tornado, spinning up through the smoke, scattering into the flames.

Virgil thought he was dying. He cried out for his mother. "Mom!" he shouted. "Help me, Mom!"

She was there.

"Hush, little baby," she said. "Don't you cry."

She dug through the dirt. She crawled into the ground and lay on top of him, to shield him from the heat.

"Sleep now," she said.

And he did.

49

The Sasquatch

When Virgil woke up, everything was silent. He pushed away the dirt and came up from the ground. The wooden box was charred and broken, the little brass plate so blackened that Virgil couldn't make out his mother's name.

Everywhere, the ground was hot and smoking. Through the forest drifted little skeins of smoke, while here and there a flame still burned. Everything was black and gray, and it made Virgil think of pictures of Passchendaele and Blenheim Wood, of old battlefields left in smoldering ruins.

The wind had gone, and the silence seemed wonderful. The dead forest felt peaceful and still.

Too sore to move, Virgil just lay there. His leg ached worse then ever, and he was afraid his back was burned. He didn't believe he could get up and walk away, but the fire was over and he was glad for that.

He turned his head just enough to look up at the sky. He saw clouds, puffy and white, and the sun shining between them.

In the quiet of the forest, he heard a sound that amazed him. The chatter of a squirrel. He looked toward it and saw the animal peering out from a hole in a blackened tree. It quivered as it shouted at him. Then, suddenly, it pulled back and disappeared into the tree.

Virgil smiled. He wasn't the only survivor. The whole forest, he thought, would live again.

When he heard a crackling among the trees, he raised his head to look, thinking the squirrel had come back.

There was something moving among the trees, something partly hidden by the smoke and branches. It walked on two feet, and with every step the ground crunched underneath it.

A Sasquatch, thought Virgil.

He lay dead still, afraid to stare straight at the creature in case it sensed him there.

It disappeared in the smoke, as though fading away. Virgil could hear it moving but couldn't see it. Then it emerged again, and stopped.

It was holding a branch or a stick, and something bristled from its back. But it kept changing shape in Virgil's eyes as the smoke flurried around the clearing. It faded away and brightened again, a thing with a black snout and a big round head. Slowly, it turned to look at him.

Virgil pressed his face into the charred ground. He smelled charcoal and ash, and he heard the creature walking toward him.

50

Carried Away

Virgil didn't have enough strength to get up and run away. He wasn't sure he could even dig himself out from the ground. He just lay facedown in the burned forest, hoping the thing hadn't seen him.

Its feet crunched on charcoal and ash. Virgil pictured them in his mind, huge and hairy, soles as thick as leather, pressing a hollow into the ground with each step. It came slowly at first, and then suddenly faster. When it stopped, Virgil knew it was right beside him.

But he heard it breathing, air whooshing in and out. With a crackling sound, it shifted on the burned grass.

A hand brushed away the dirt that lay on top of him. A voice said, "Oh no. You poor kid."

Virgil turned his head. The hand flew away, and the voice said, "Holy crap, you're alive!"

Virgil opened his eyes. Instead of hairy Sasquatch feet,

he saw a pair of black boots laced to the top and heavy pants with quilted legs. He looked higher—up at a big leather belt, up again at a face covered by goggles and a rubber mask, up once more at the hard helmet of a firefighter. He opened his mouth, but it was hard to speak. He said, "Hi."

The firefighter put down the sprayer that he carried and shrugged the water tank from his back. He pulled off his helmet and dropped it on the ground. It landed upside down, like half a watermelon, rocking back and forth. He shook off his gloves and tore off his mask, shedding them all in a moment.

The man's face was black with soot, making his eyes look huge and startled. He opened his mouth and shouted, "Come help me! There's a kid lying here. He's alive!"

He scraped away the rest of the dirt, clawing it back with his hands, digging down to the mud. "Is someone with you?" he asked.

"No," said Virgil.

"I couldn't tell for sure," said the firefighter. "It looked like someone was standing right over you. I was sure of it. But you see strange things in the smoke sometimes."

He slipped his hands under Virgil and lifted the boy from the ground. He carried him away, through the ashes of the Beast, still shouting for someone to help him.

51

Ashes to Ashes

Virgil fell asleep in the fireman's arms, his head tipped back and his mouth wide open. When he woke up, he was lying in a hospital bed with a plastic mask over his mouth, tubes running in and out of him, his family all around.

He saw Kaitlyn first. She was perched on the edge of a chair with a crutch leaning against it. Beside her sat Joshua, his face scratched and bug-bitten, smeared in shiny ointment. "*Hola*," he said, holding up a hand. "*Bienvenido.*"

Then Virgil turned his head a little more and saw his father sitting on the other side, reaching out just then toward him. His dad touched his forehead and started crying.

"Aww, Dad," said Kaitlyn. "We're going to be all right."

"I know," he said. "I'm just happy." Through his tears, he sort of laughed. "I'm so proud of you all."

"We look like the walking wounded," said Joshua.

It was true. When Kaitlyn got up, she hobbled around the room like an old pirate with a wooden leg, every step marked by a tap from her crutch and a thump from the cast round her ankle. Joshua looked as though he'd been wrestling cats. But Virgil was the worst. He had bandages around his arms and legs, and the doctors had said it would take a long time for his burns to heal. They'd said he was very lucky to be alive.

Virgil didn't agree. It wasn't luck that had saved him; it was the things he had learned from his mom. But, still, he kept thinking of the firefighter scraping through smoldering dirt, certain that he'd seen two people. "It looked like someone was standing right over you." It gave Virgil goose bumps just to think about it, and he loved the idea that his mom had been watching over him, keeping him safe as flames swept past all around him. But he wasn't so sure it was true. The man might have seen a curl of smoke, or a twisted tree standing in the fog of the fire.

He *hoped* it was true. But he decided that he would never tell anyone what the firefighter had seen. People would laugh, he thought. They would shake their heads and say, "No, that's impossible." He had a feeling, in a circular way he couldn't sort out, that his mom would have told him that.

Then he found himself alone with Kaitlyn. It was late in the day, and Joshua and his dad had gone for dinner. Kaitlyn got down from her chair to kneel beside his bed. Her face was just inches from his. "I gotta ask you, Virg," she said. "What happened to Mom's ashes?"

She had heard most of the story. Virgil had told her how he'd crashed the van and fled through the forest, how he'd seen the mountain lion and missed the helicopter. He had told her what had happened at the Sasquatch museum and how he'd nearly died at the cliff. She knew how he'd dug himself into the ground. But she hadn't asked till then what had happened to the ashes. Nobody had asked him that.

"I forgot the box at first," he said. "But I went back and got it, and then I carried it everywhere. I wrapped it up in a bundle."

Kaitlyn's fingers plucked at the sheet like a cat's claws, pulling it up into little tents. She stared right into his eyes.

"At the end I lay down in the ground and held onto the box," said Virgil. "It was broken, but all the ashes were still inside. Then the wind from the fire started pulling them out, and I couldn't stop it. They blew away. Into the forest."

"Ashes to ashes," said Kaitlyn.

Virgil nodded.

"Mom would like that."

Satisfied, Kaitlyn began to pull away. She arranged her crutch to lever herself back up again. Virgil almost let her go without saying another word. Lying on his back, looking up at the ceiling, he blurted out, "She was there."

Kaitlyn stopped. "What do you mean?"

"She was there," said Virgil again. "I don't know if it's true, or if I just dreamed it, but it was like she was there."

"Well, of course she was there, Virg," said Kaitlyn. "She'll always be looking after you."

"I mean really," said Virgil. "Not just her spirit or

something. She was actually there, keeping me safe." Behind his bed, a machine was softly beeping, flashing lights of red and green. "Do you think that's dumb?"

"No," said Kaitlyn. "I believe it, Virg."

Virgil could feel Kaitlyn watching him, but he kept staring up at the ceiling. "Mom was great," he said.

Kaitlyn smiled. "Mom was the best."

Virgil dreamed of his mom that night. He was standing at the shore of Little Lost Lake, and the wooden box was in his hands. The fire had never happened. But all the animals that he and Kaitlyn had seen go by on the Boneyard were there in his dream. They came parading from the forest on the far side of the lake, gathering quietly along the shore. Birds swarmed from the sky to fill every tree, while bears and squirrels, deer and mice, raccoons and beavers and elk lined themselves along the shore. They sat, or they stood, or they lay themselves down at the water's edge. Even the mountain lion was there, gliding from the bushes to take its place between a rabbit and a deer. They looked at Virgil but made no sound.

In his dream, he opened the box. Out came a swirl of gray dust that shaped itself into his mom, just the same as she had looked in the halls of the school, as happy and healthy as ever.

She smiled at him; she touched him, then she turned and walked away. She stepped from the grass to the dry mud at the shore and straight out onto Little Lost Lake. A few yards from shore, she dissolved again into the little cloud of ashes. It shimmered in the sun and floated away like the down of a dandelion.

Virgil woke then with a feeling of loneliness. Through his open door he heard hospital sounds: the beeping of machines and the wheeling of a cart down the hall, the soft squish from the shoes of the nurse that pushed it. He had no feeling that his mom had been there in his room, the way she had been with him in the forest. He knew he'd only been dreaming. But he felt that she had gone now.

Only a week earlier, that thought would have filled Virgil with fear. But now he knew he could go on without his mother, if he held onto the things she'd taught him. "No matter how bad the storm, it always gets sunny again," she had said. He hadn't believed her at the time, but she was right even about that. The storm inside him was passing over.